TIGER MOTH
Insect Ninja

Librarian Reviewer
Diane R. Chen
Library Information Specialist,
Hickman Elementary, Nashville, TN
MA in LIS, University of Iowa
BA El Ed & Modern Languages/Chinese,
Buena Vista University

Reading Consultant
Mark DeYoung
Classroom Teacher, Edina Public Schools, MN
BA in Elementary Education, Central College
MS in Curriculum & Instruction, University of Minnesota

STONE ARCH BOOKS
MINNEAPOLIS SAN DIEGO

Graphic Sparks are published by Stone Arch Books,
151 Good Counsel Drive, P.O. Box 669,
Mankato, Minnesota 56002.
www.stonearchbooks.com

Library of Congress Cataloging-in-Publication Data
Reynolds, Aaron, 1970–
    Tiger Moth, Insect Ninja / by Aaron Reynolds; illustrated by Eric Lervold.
    p. cm. — (Graphic Sparks. Tiger Moth)
    ISBN-13: 978-1-59889-057-0 (hardcover)
    ISBN-10: 1-59889-057-3 (hardcover)
    ISBN-13: 978-1-59889-228-4 (paperback)
    ISBN-10: 1-59889-228-2 (paperback)
    1. Graphic novels. I. Lervold, Eric. II. Title. III. Series: Reynolds, Aaron, 1970–
Graphic Sparks. Tiger Moth.
PN6727.R45I58 2007
741.5'973—dc22   2006007700

Summary: Young Tiger Moth is a ninja-in-training, a martial arts warrior who fights
evil in the streets and classrooms of the bug world. With the help of his best
friend, pillbug Kung Pow, he works for truth and justice, while still hoping to finish
the 4th grade.

Art Director: Heather Kindseth
Designer: Keegan Gilbert

1 2 3 4 5 6 11 10 09 08 07 06

Printed in the United States of America

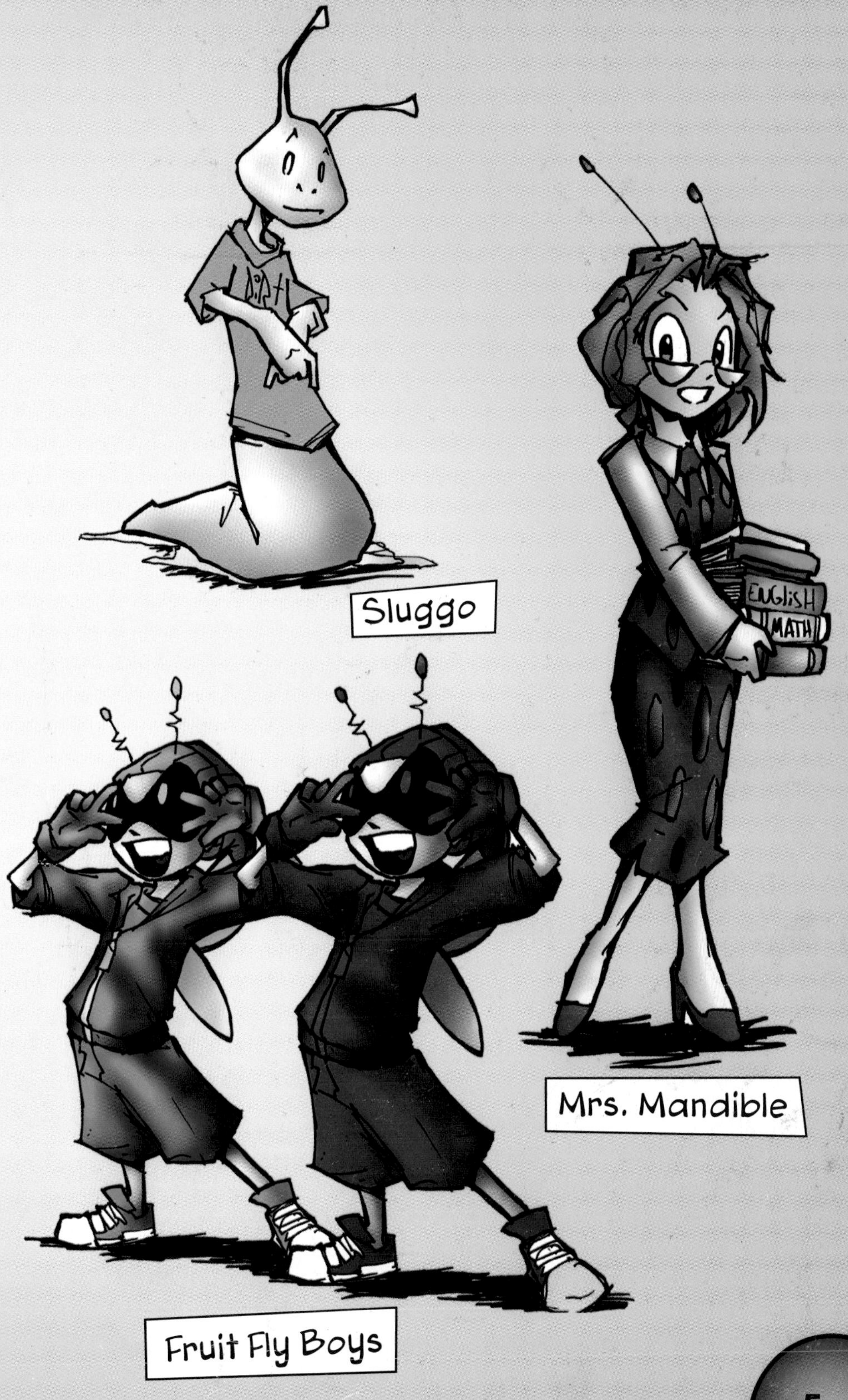
DIRT
Sluggo
ENGLISH
MATH
Mrs. Mandible
Fruit Fly Boys

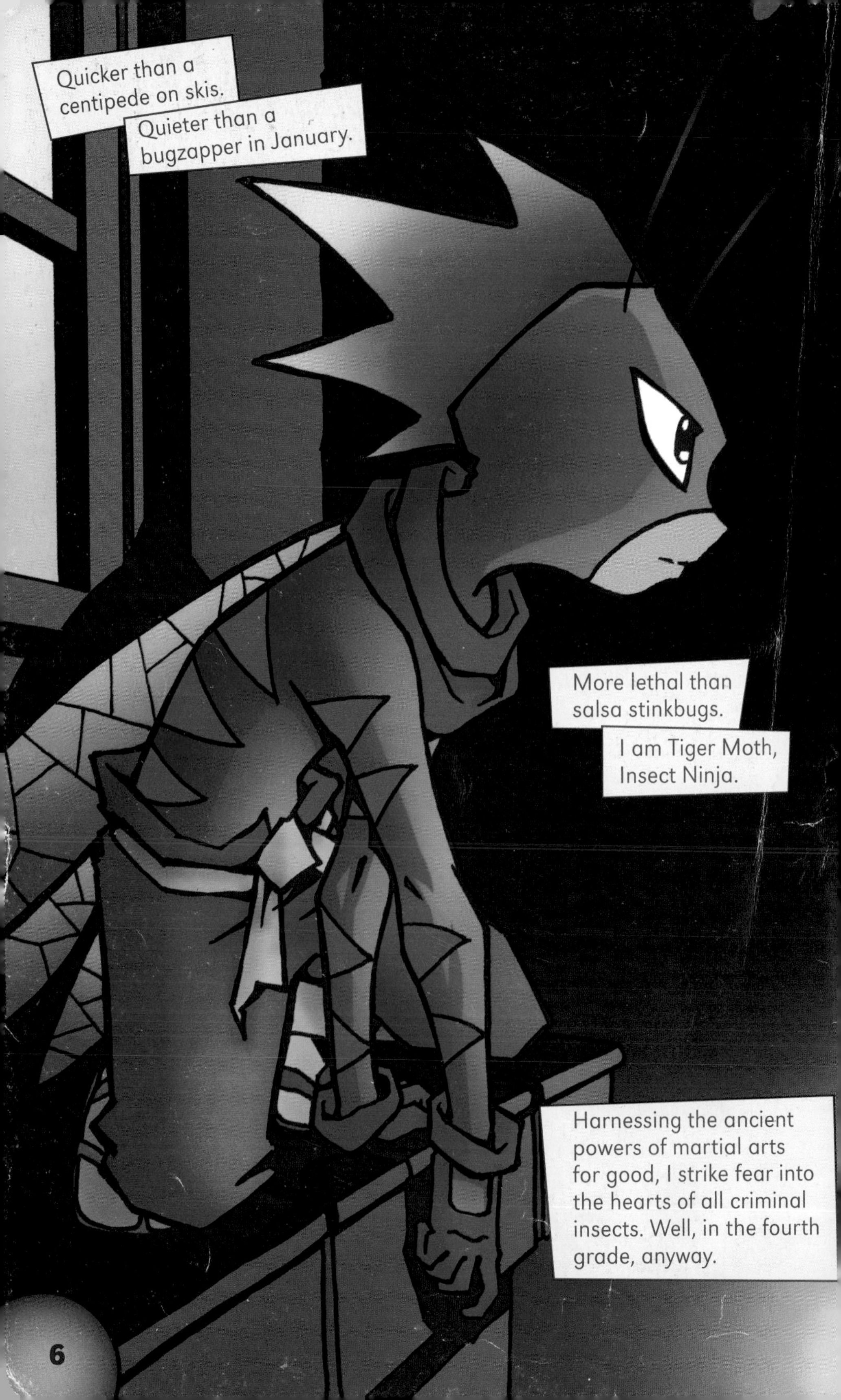

Quicker than a
centipede on skis.
Quieter than a
bugzapper in January.
More lethal than
salsa stinkbugs.
I am Tiger Moth,
Insect Ninja.
Harnessing the ancient
powers of martial arts
for good, I strike fear into
the hearts of all criminal
insects. Well, in the fourth
grade, anyway.

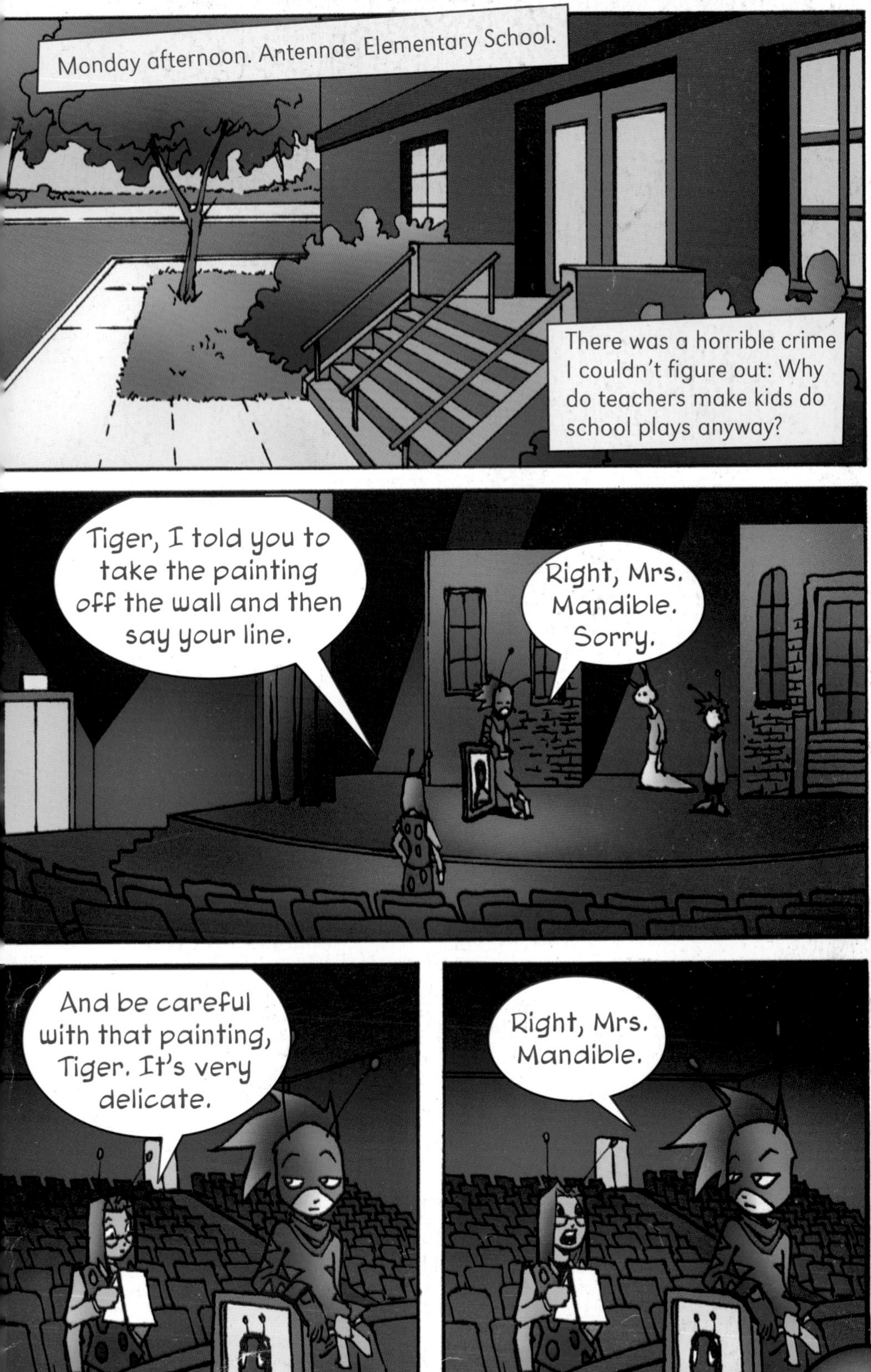

Monday afternoon. Antennae Elementary School.
There was a horrible crime I couldn't figure out: Why do teachers make kids do school plays anyway?
Tiger, I told you to take the painting off the wall and then say your line.
Right, Mrs. Mandible. Sorry.
And be careful with that painting, Tiger. It's very delicate.
Right, Mrs. Mandible.

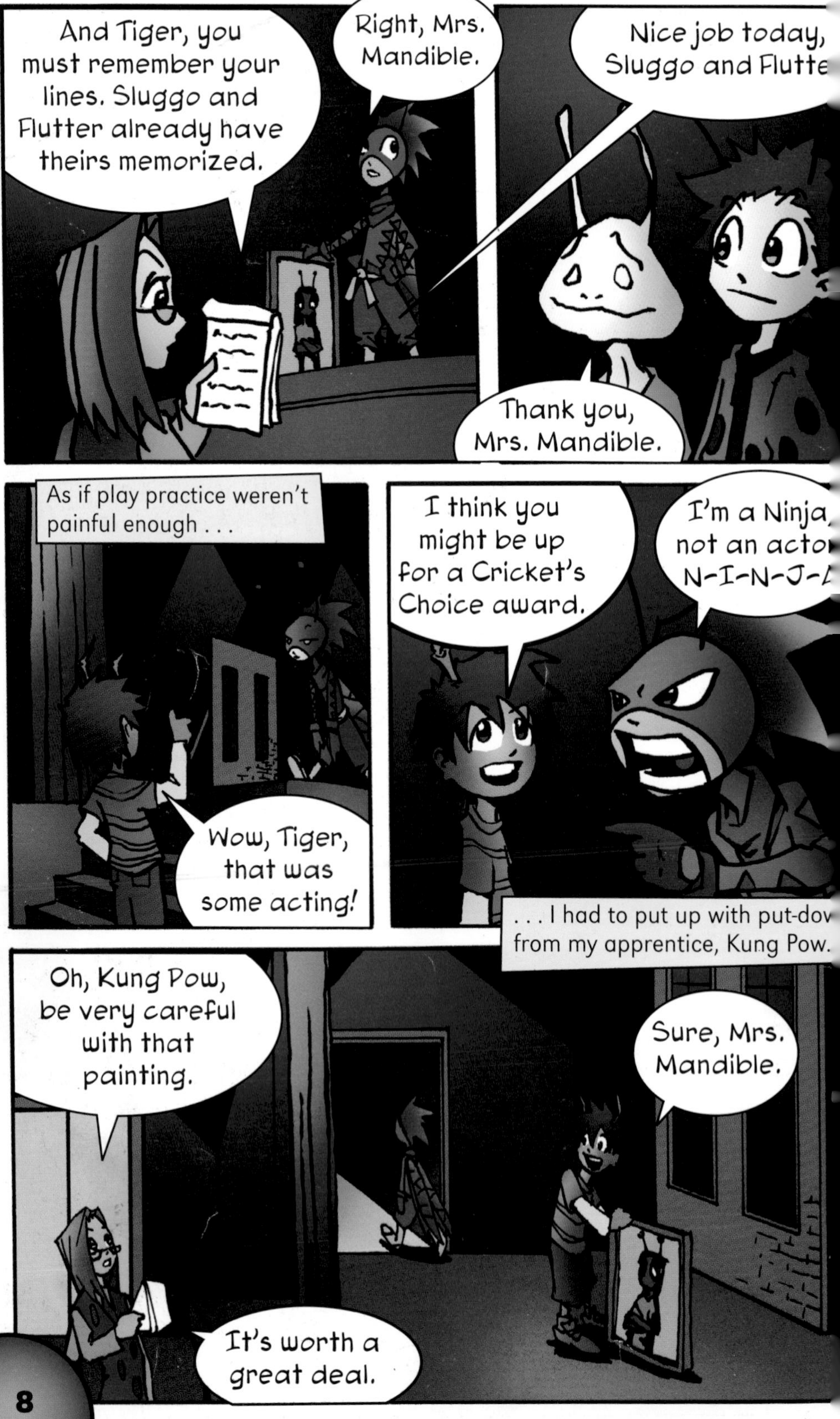

And Tiger, you must remember your lines. Sluggo and Flutter already have theirs memorized.
Right, Mrs. Mandible.
Nice job today, Sluggo and Flutte
Thank you, Mrs. Mandible.
As if play practice weren't painful enough . . .
Wow, Tiger, that was some acting!
I think you might be up for a Cricket's Choice award.
I'm a Ninja, not an acto N-I-N-J-
. . . I had to put up with put-dov from my apprentice, Kung Pow.
Oh, Kung Pow, be very careful with that painting.
It's worth a great deal.
Sure, Mrs. Mandible.

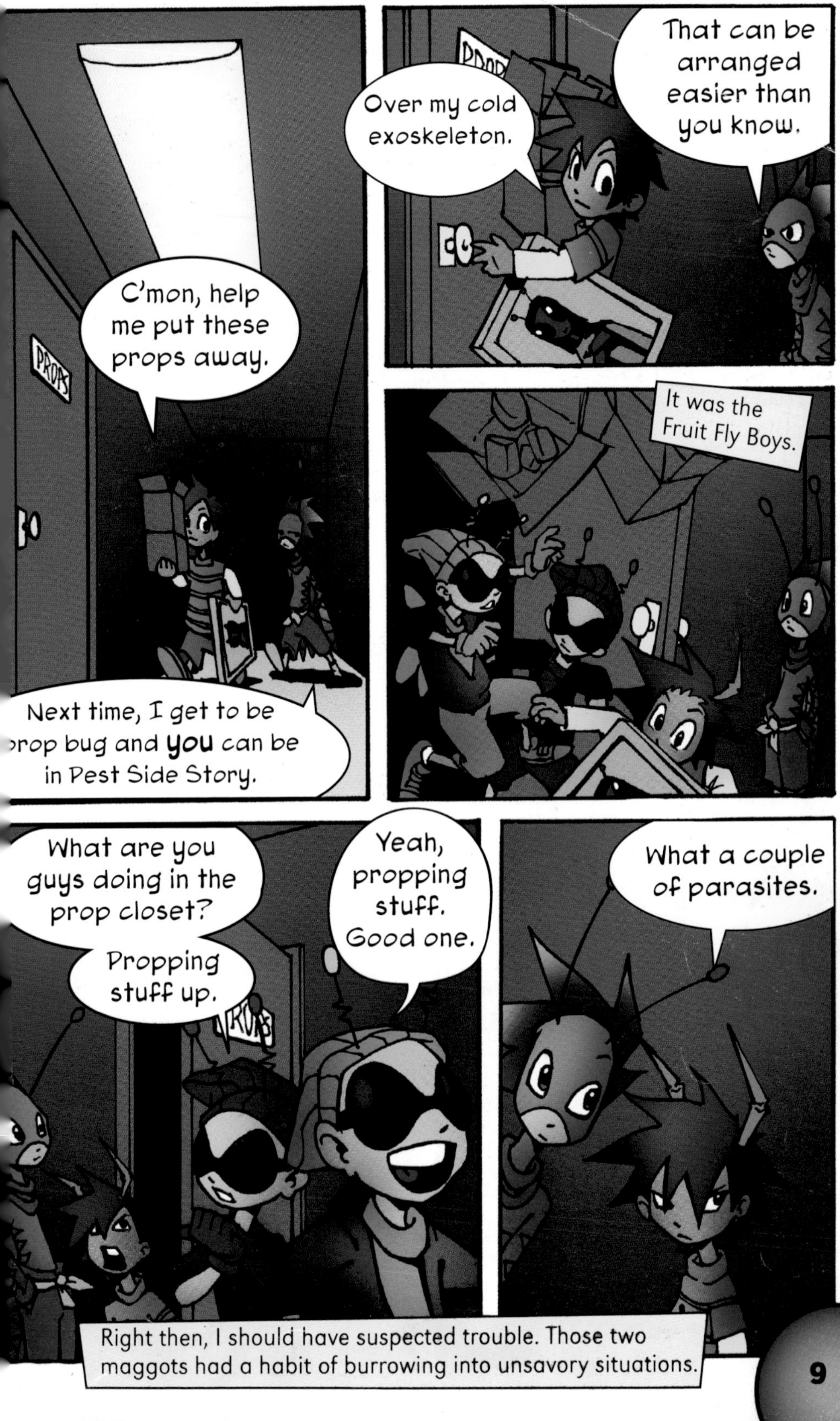
PROPS
C'mon, help me put these props away.
Next time, I get to be
rop bug and you can be
in Pest Side Story.
Over my cold exoskeleton.
That can be arranged easier than you know.
It was the Fruit Fly Boys.
What are you guys doing in the prop closet?
Propping stuff up.
Yeah, propping stuff. Good one.
What a couple of parasites.
Right then, I should have suspected trouble. Those two maggots had a habit of burrowing into unsavory situations.

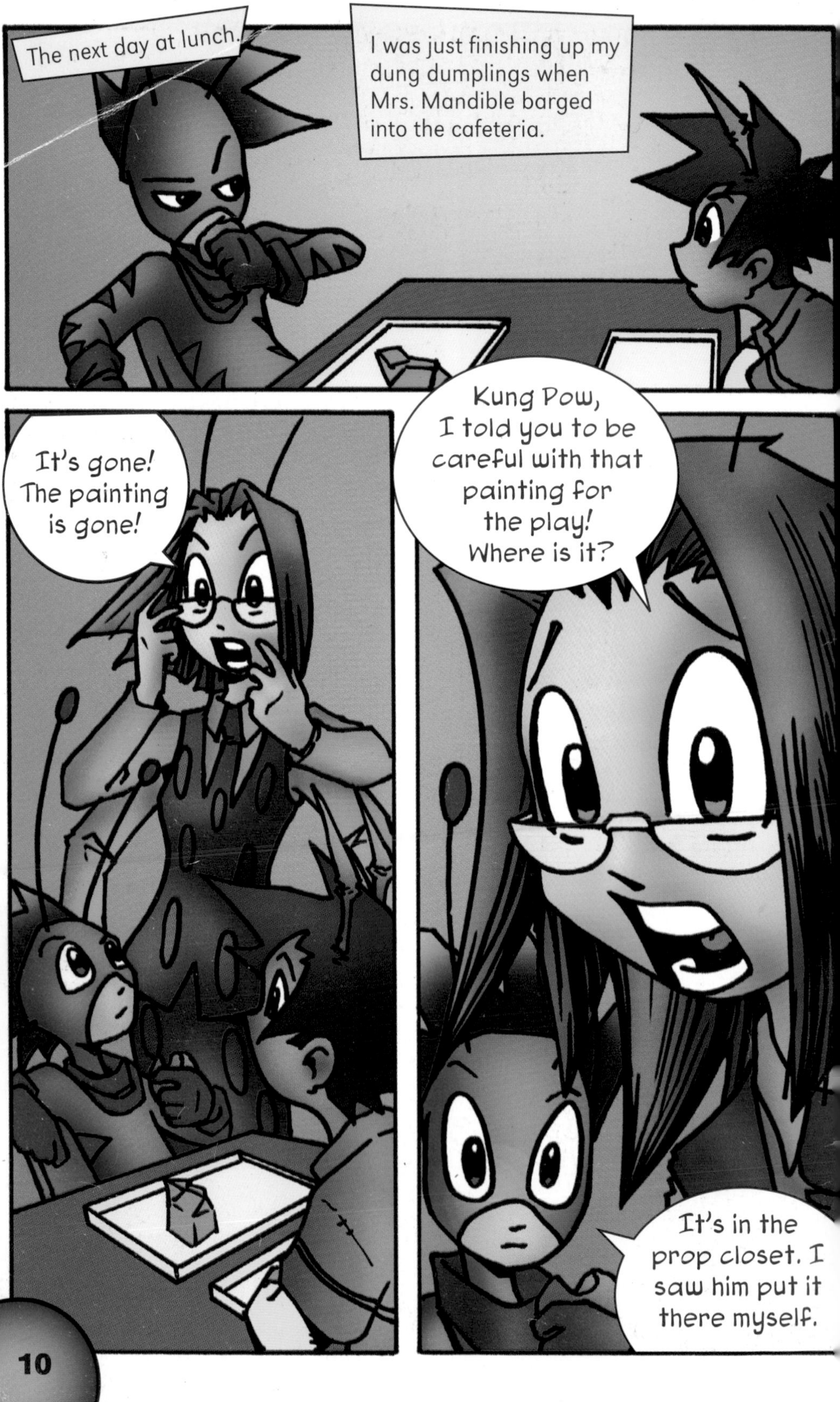
The next day at lunch.
I was just finishing up my dung dumplings when Mrs. Mandible barged into the cafeteria.
It's gone! The painting is gone!
Kung Pow, I told you to be careful with that painting for the play! Where is it?
It's in the prop closet. I saw him put it there myself.

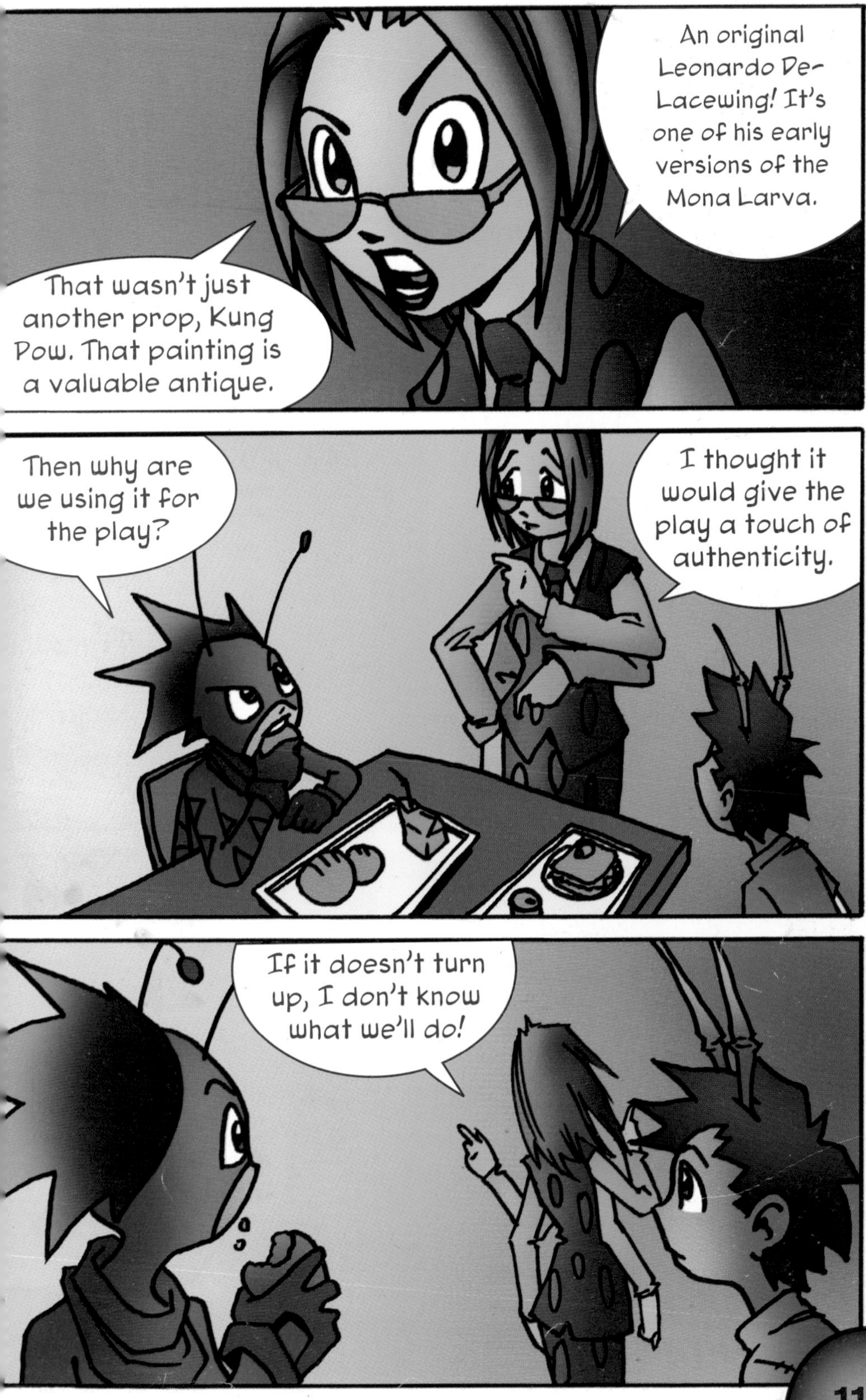
An original Leonardo De-Lacewing! It's one of his early versions of the Mona Larva.
That wasn't just another prop, Kung Pow. That painting is a valuable antique.
Then why are we using it for the play?
I thought it would give the play a touch of authenticity.
If it doesn't turn up, I don't know what we'll do!

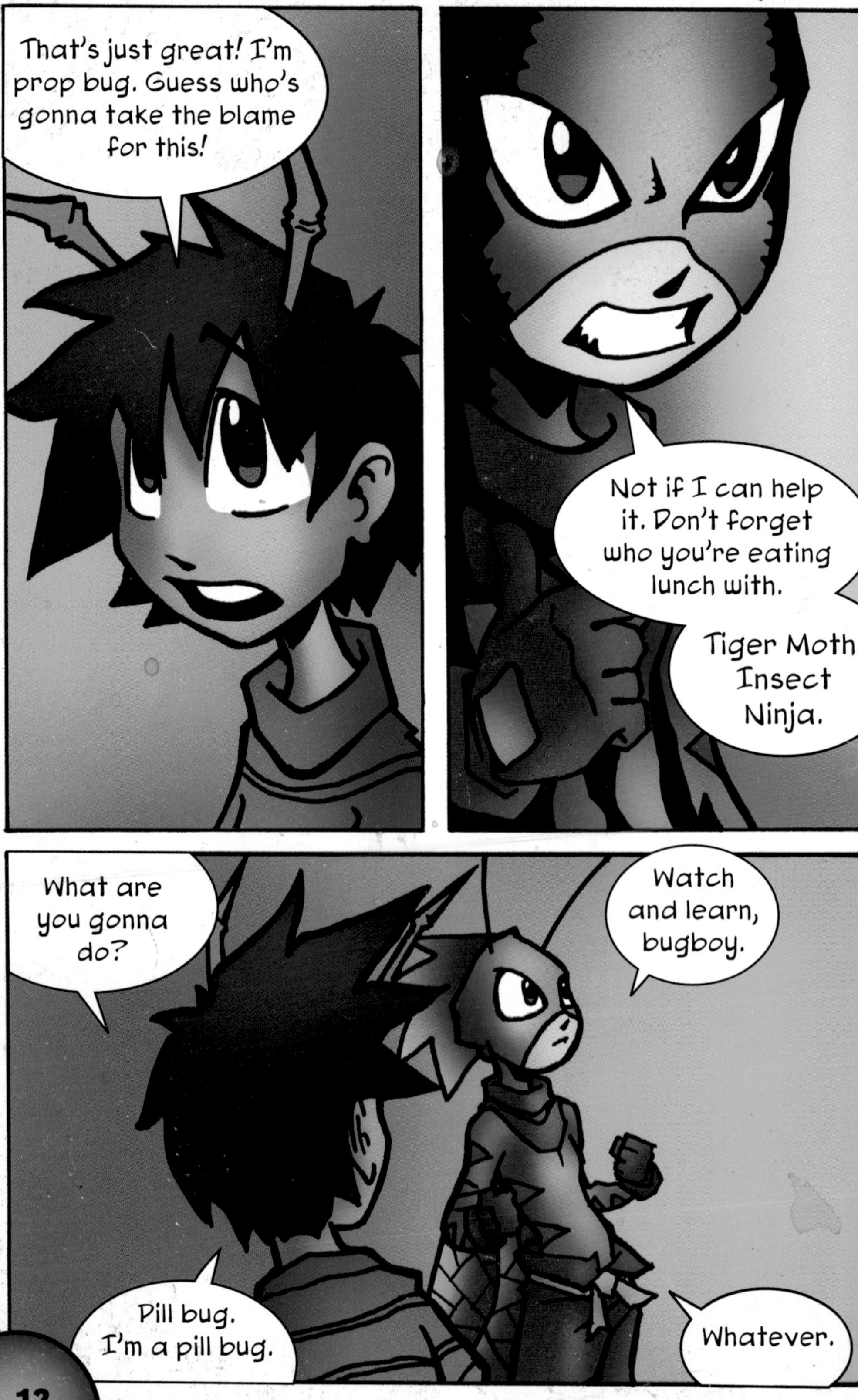

That's just great! I'm prop bug. Guess who's gonna take the blame for this!
Not if I can help it. Don't forget who you're eating lunch with.
Tiger Moth: Insect Ninja.
What are you gonna do?
Watch and learn, bugboy.
Pill bug. I'm a pill bug.
Whatever.

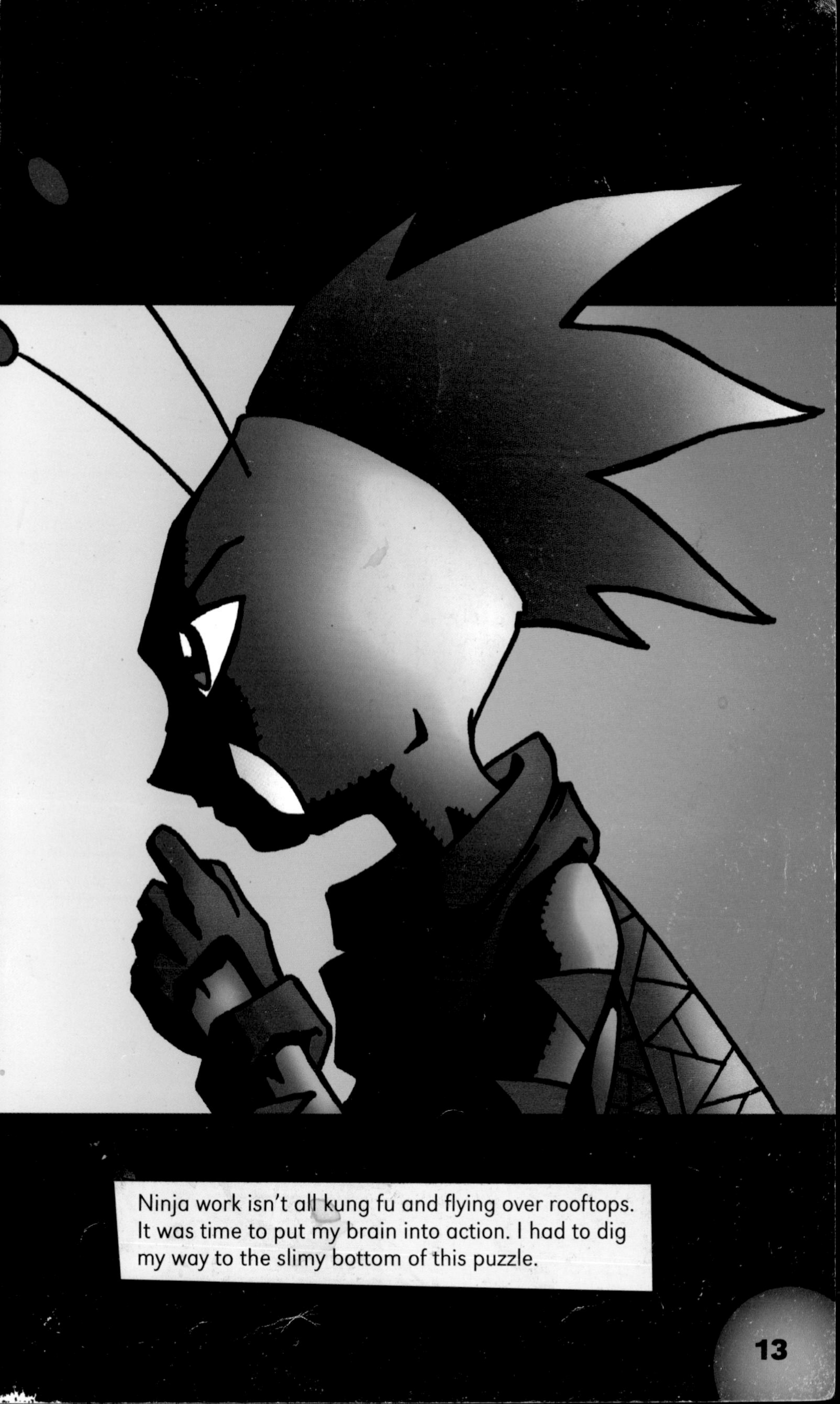

Ninja work isn't all kung fu and flying over rooftops. It was time to put my brain into action. I had to dig my way to the slimy bottom of this puzzle.

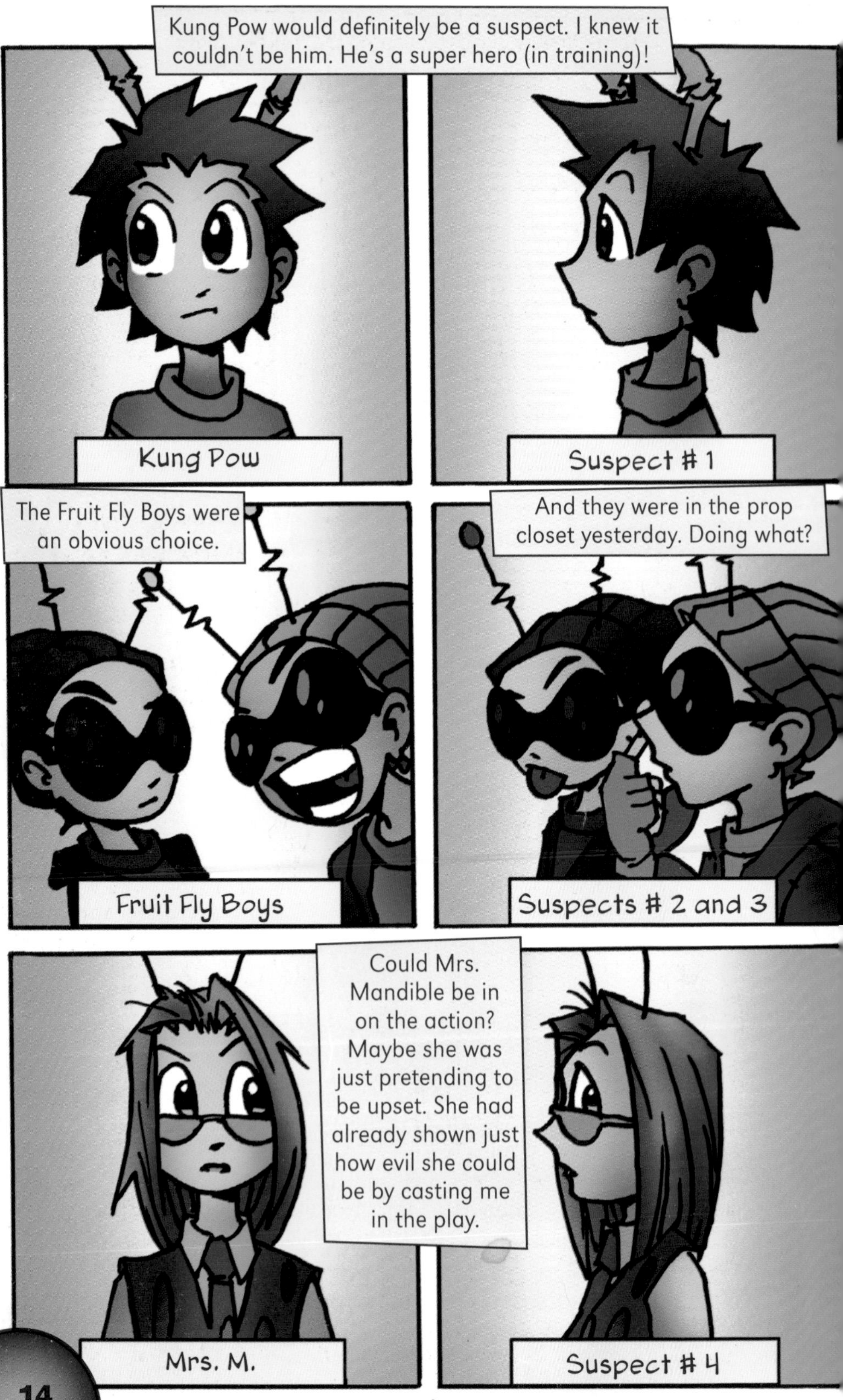

Kung Pow would definitely be a suspect. I knew it couldn't be him. He's a super hero (in training)!
Kung Pow
Suspect # 1
The Fruit Fly Boys were an obvious choice.
Fruit Fly Boys
And they were in the prop closet yesterday. Doing what?
Suspects # 2 and 3
Could Mrs. Mandible be in on the action? Maybe she was just pretending to be upset. She had already shown just how evil she could be by casting me in the play.
Mrs. M.
Suspect # 4

At recess, it was my first chance to observe the Fruit Fly Boys.

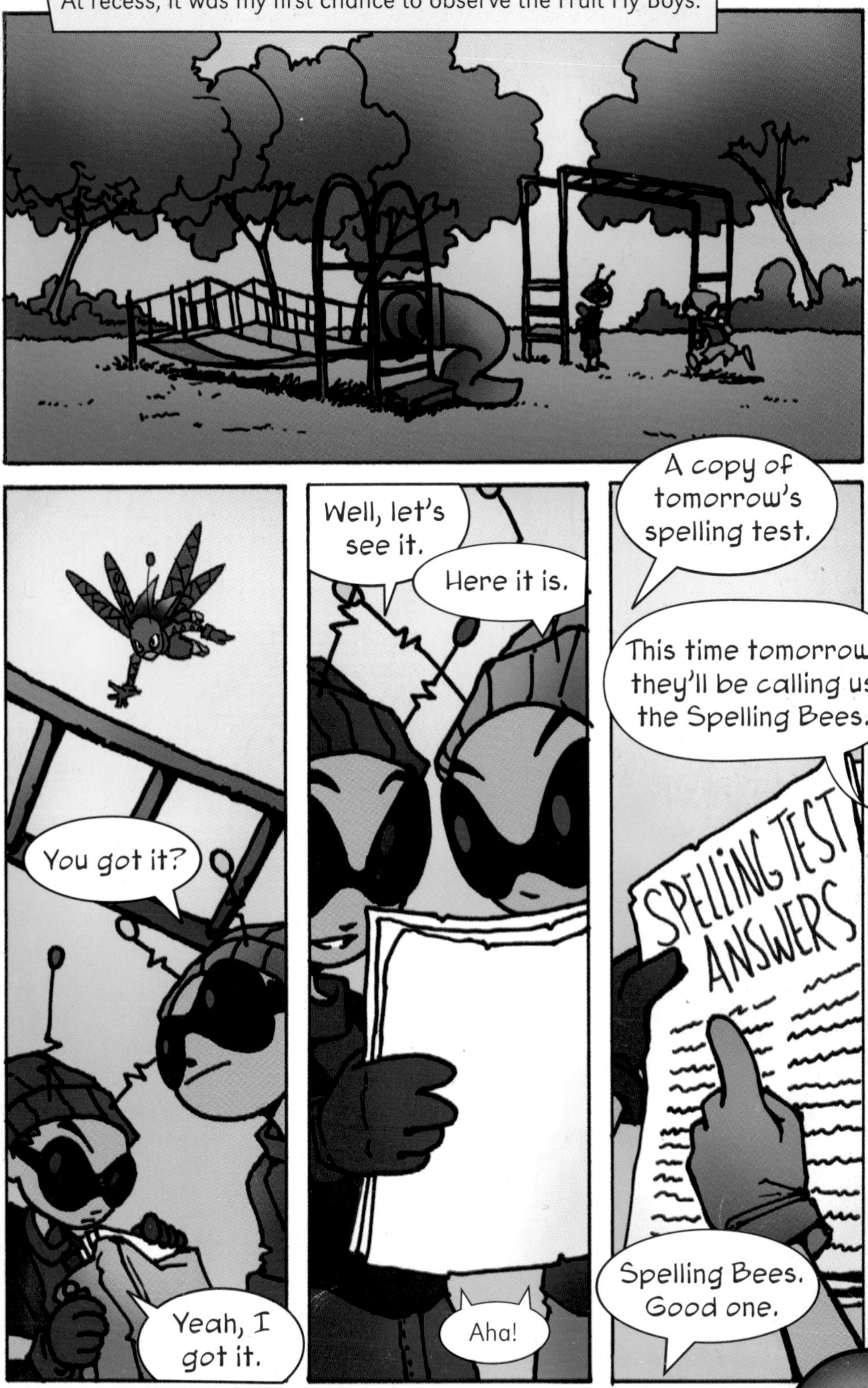

You got it?
Yeah, I got it.
Well, let's see it.
Here it is.
Aha!
A copy of tomorrow's spelling test.
This time tomorrow, they'll be calling us the Spelling Bees.
SPELLING TEST ANSWERS
Spelling Bees. Good one.

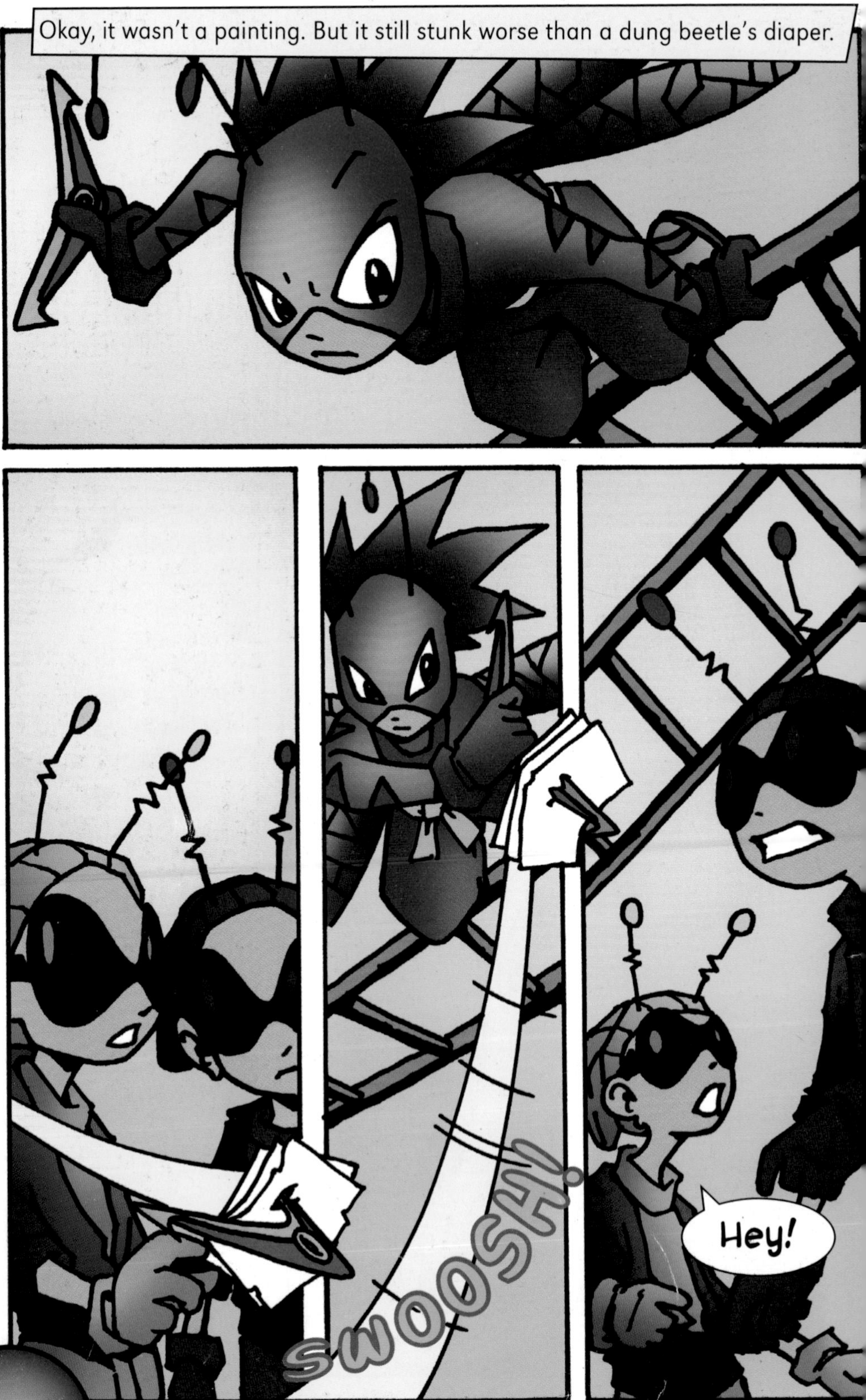
Okay, it wasn't a painting. But it still stunk worse than a dung beetle's diaper.
SWOOSH!
Hey!

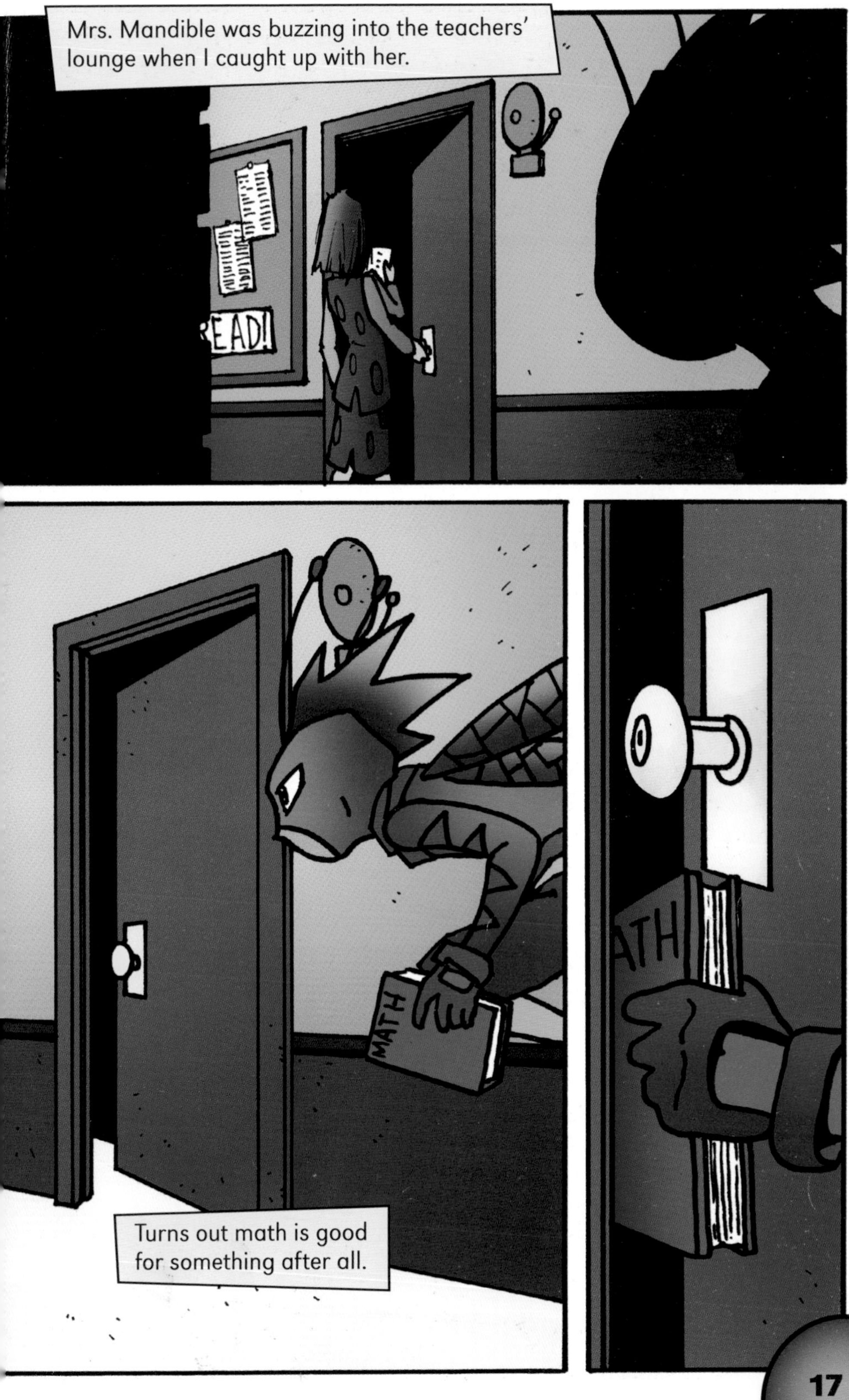

Mrs. Mandible was buzzing into the teachers' lounge when I caught up with her.
READ!
MATH
ATH
Turns out math is good for something after all.

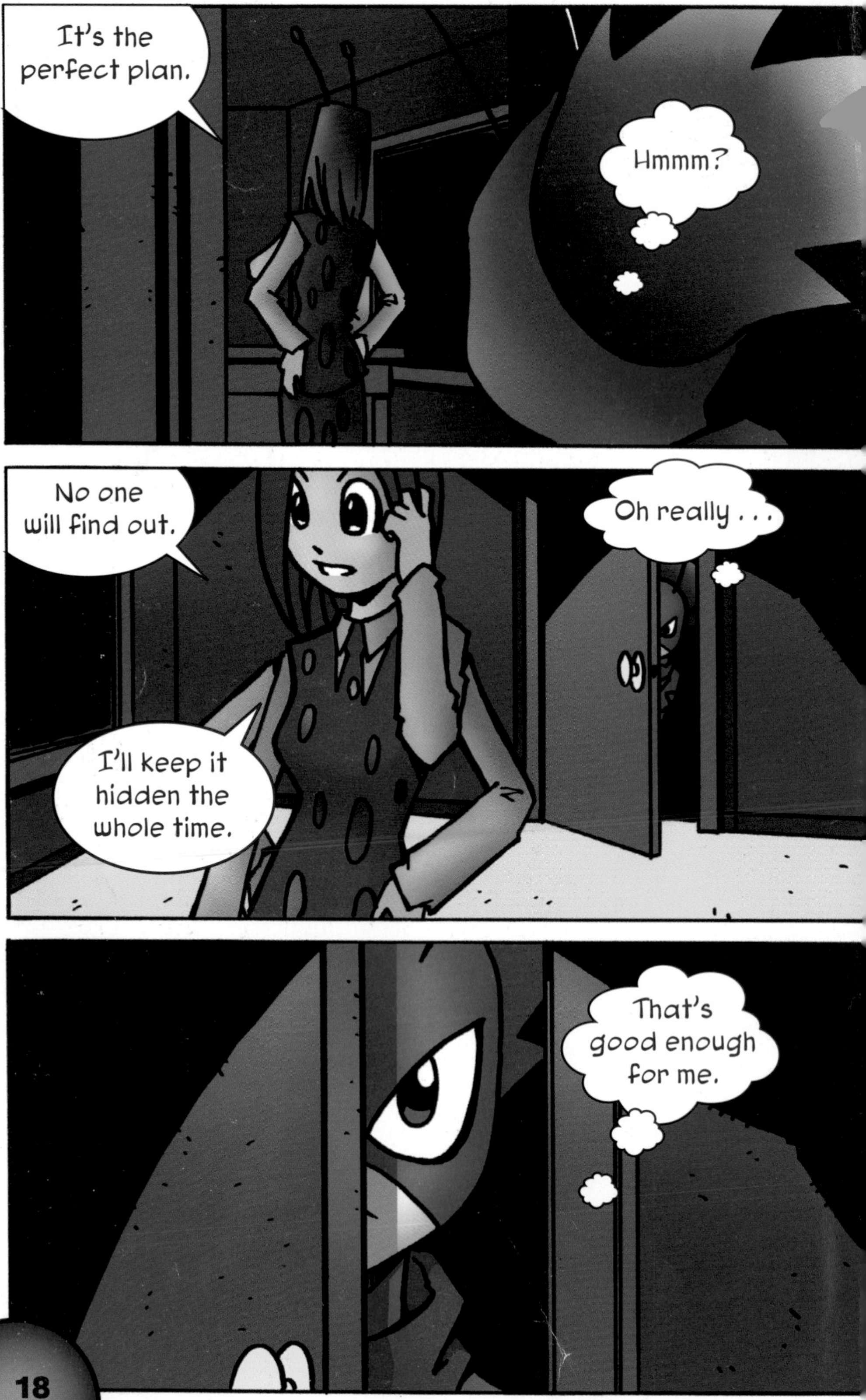
It's the perfect plan.
Hmmm?
No one will find out.
Oh really . . .
I'll keep it hidden the whole time.
That's good enough for me.

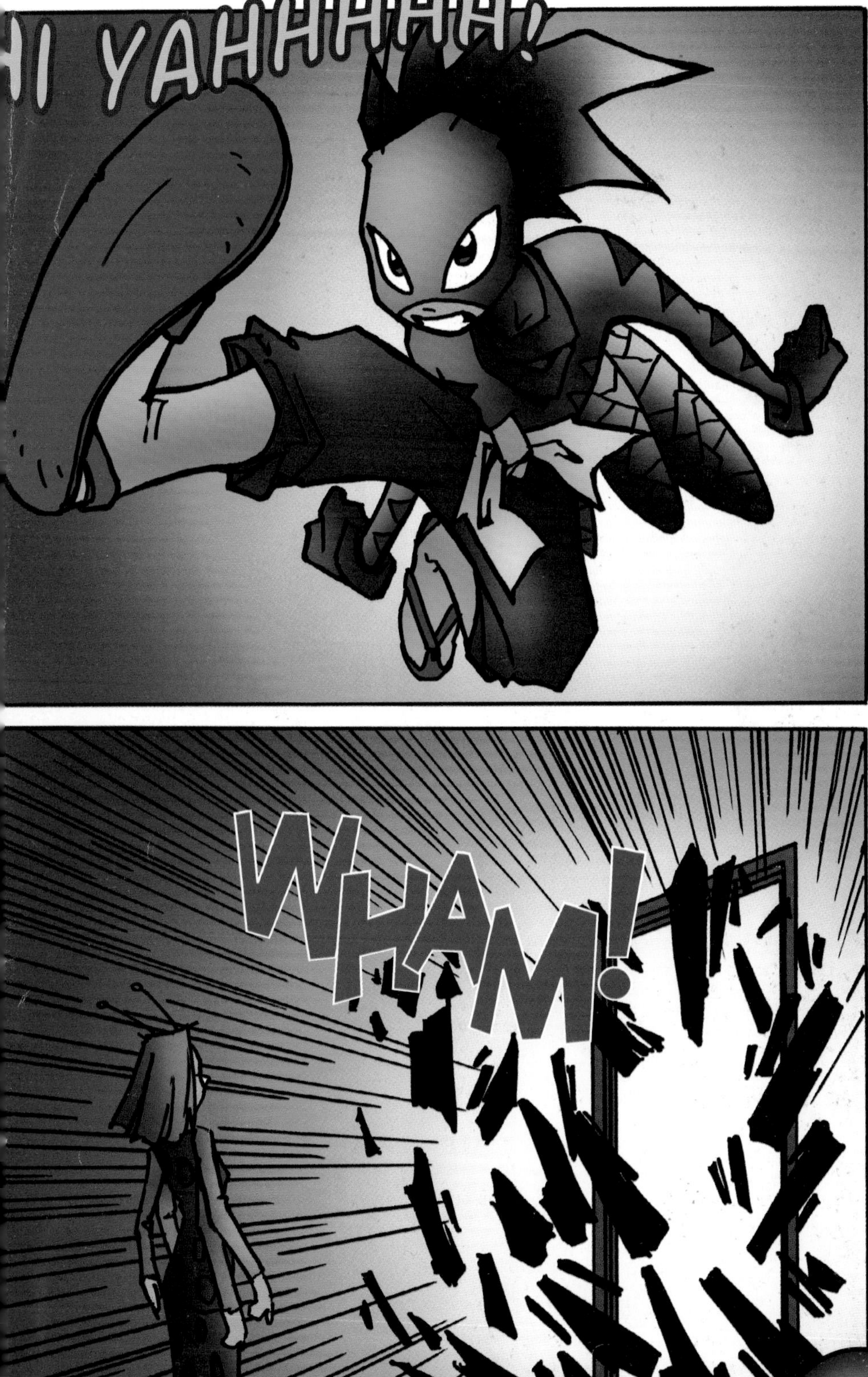
HI YAHHHHHH!
WHAM!

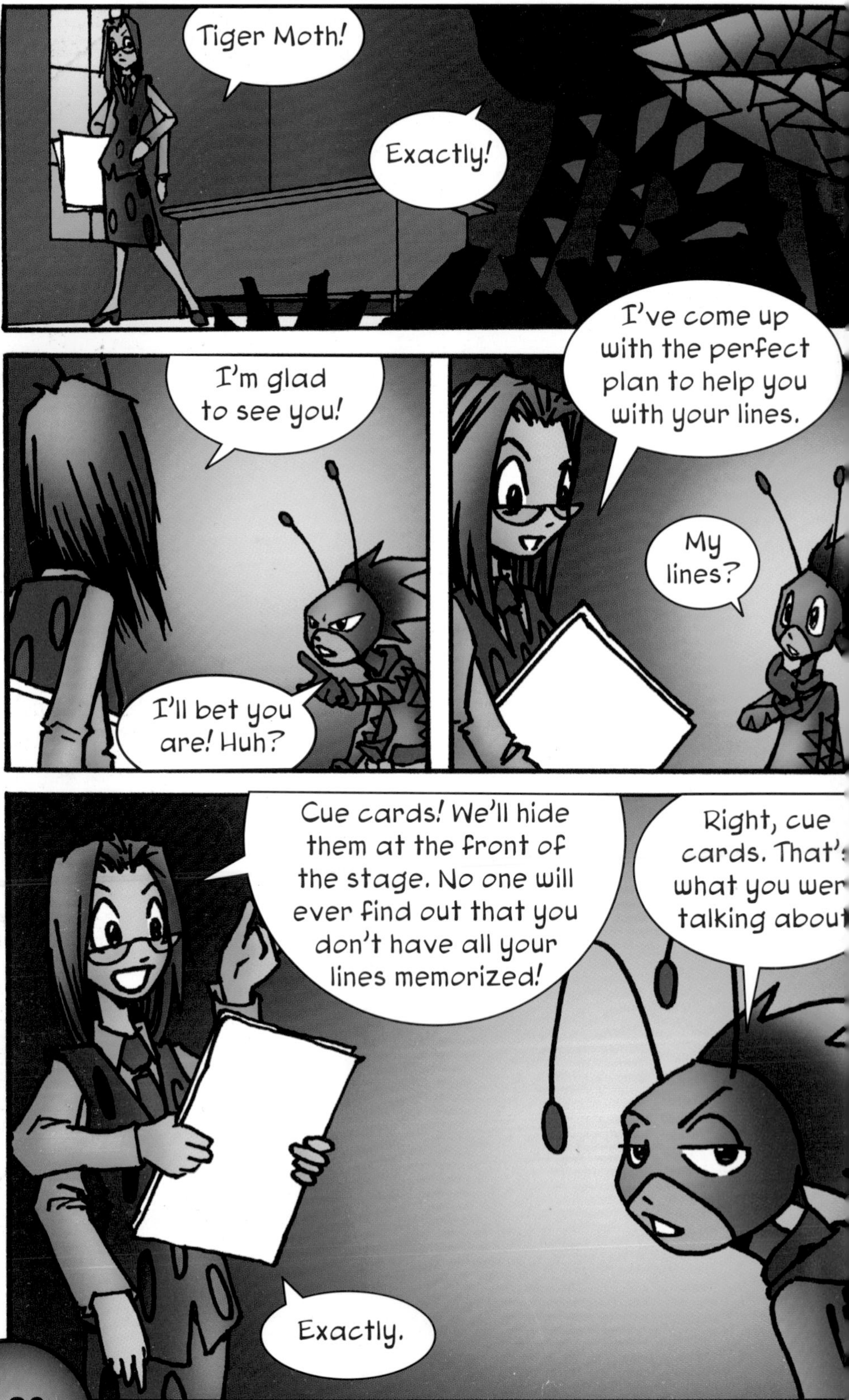
Tiger Moth!
Exactly!
I'm glad to see you!
I'll bet you are! Huh?
I've come up with the perfect plan to help you with your lines.
My lines?
Cue cards! We'll hide them at the front of the stage. No one will ever find out that you don't have all your lines memorized!
Right, cue cards. That's what you were talking about
Exactly.

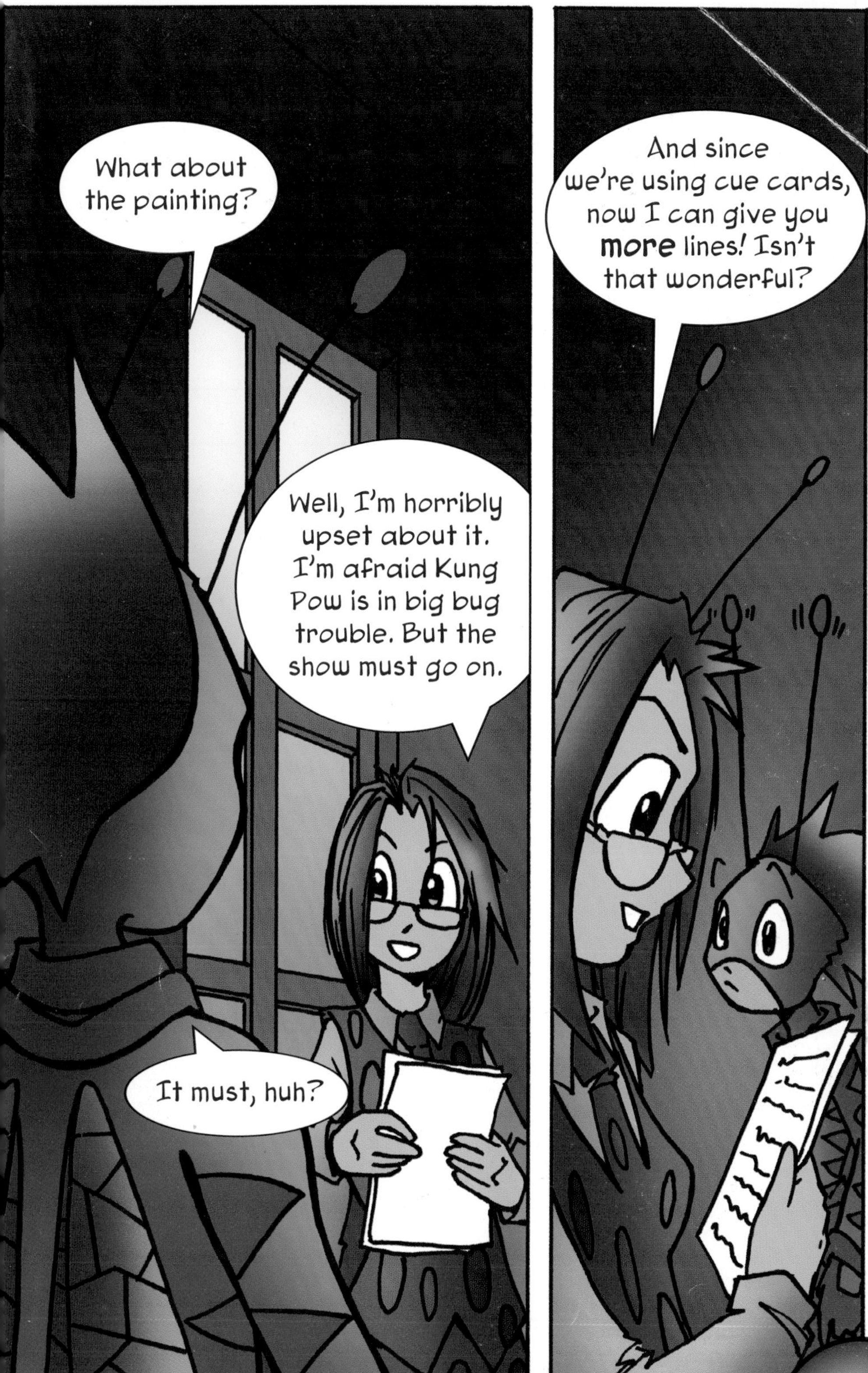

What about the painting?
Well, I'm horribly upset about it. I'm afraid Kung Pow is in big bug trouble. But the show must go on.
It must, huh?
And since we're using cue cards, now I can give you **more** lines! Isn't that wonderful?

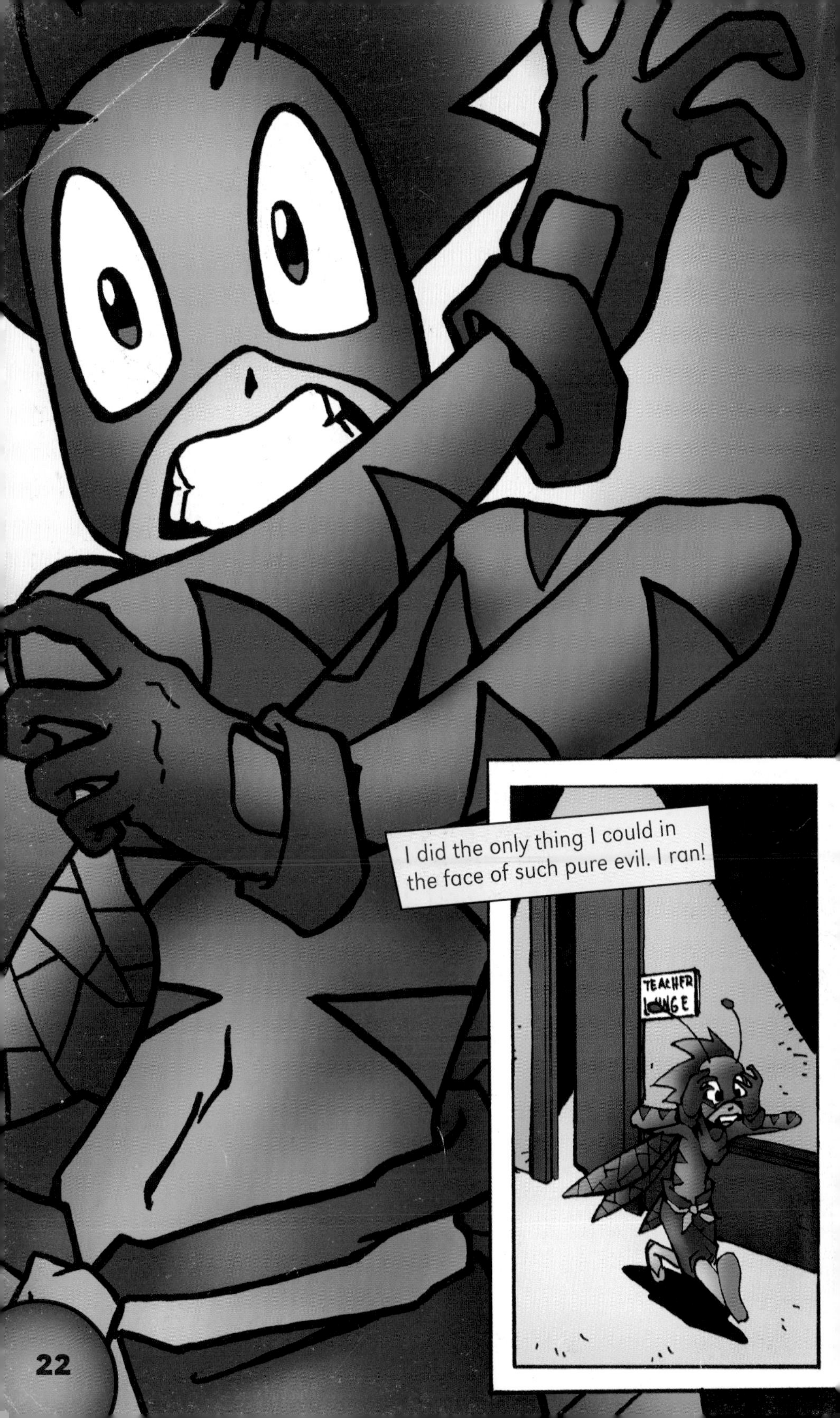
I did the only thing I could in the face of such pure evil. I ran!
TEACHER LUNGE

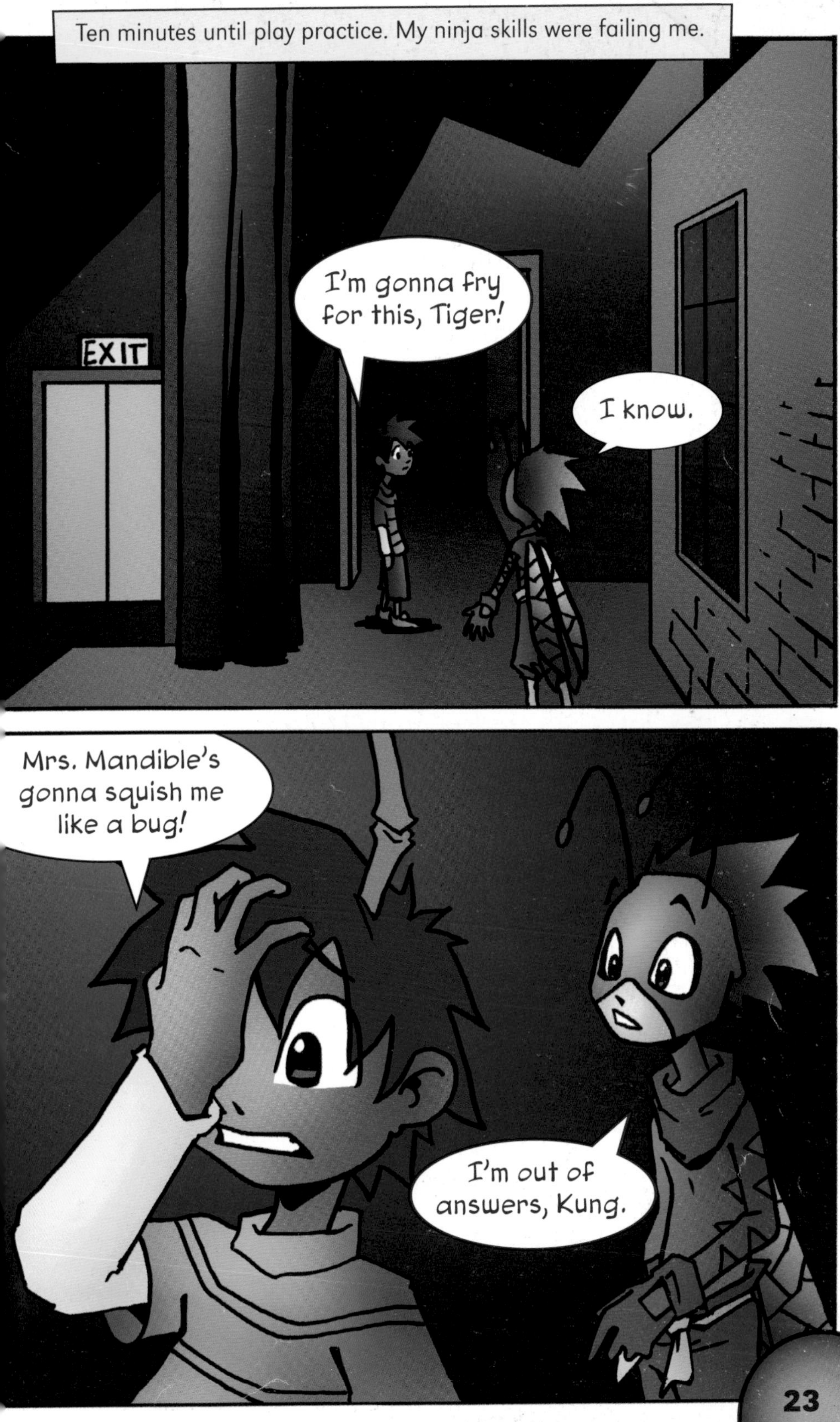
Ten minutes until play practice. My ninja skills were failing me.
EXIT
I'm gonna fry for this, Tiger!
I know.
Mrs. Mandible's gonna squish me like a bug!
I'm out of answers, Kung.

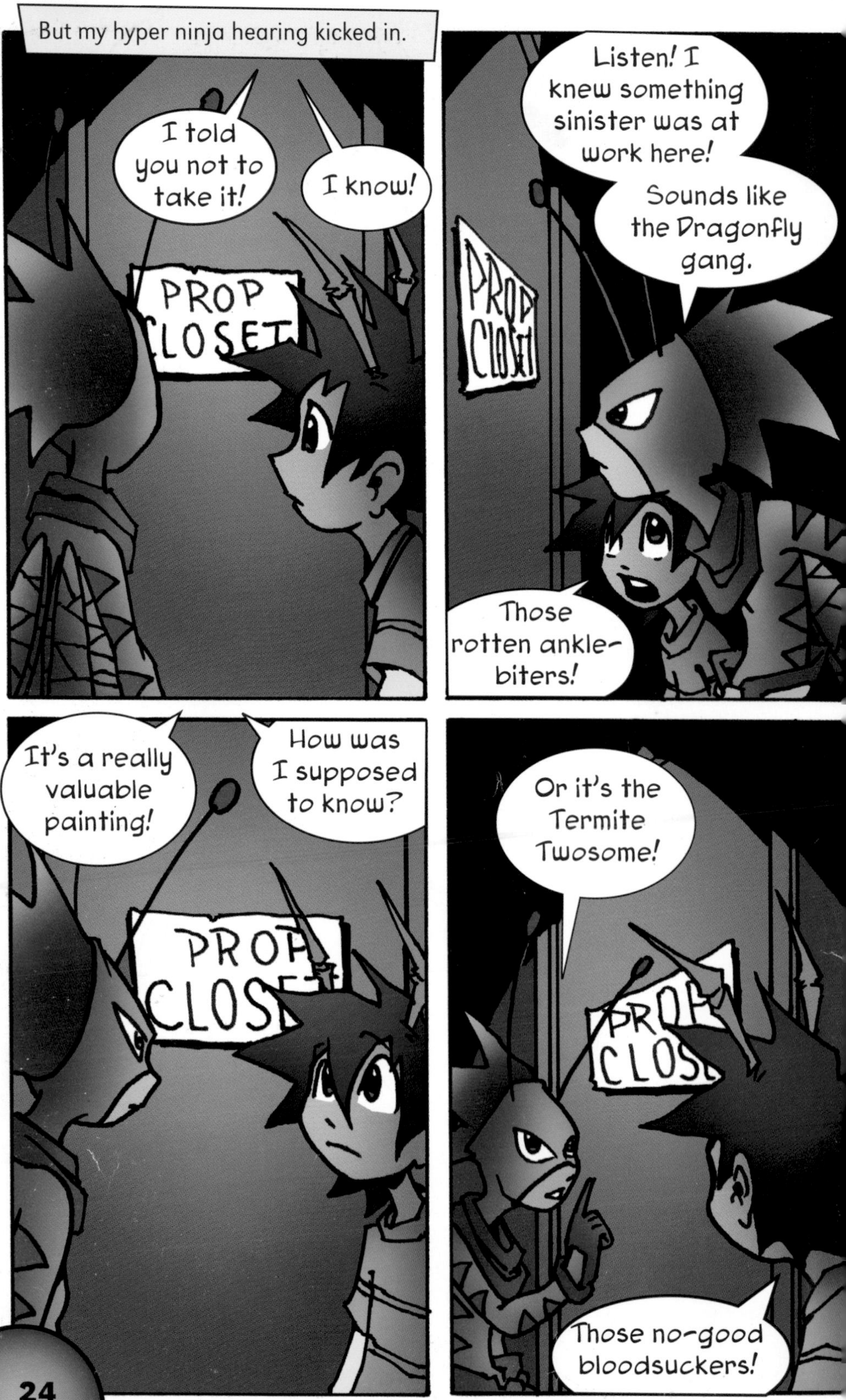
But my hyper ninja hearing kicked in.
I told you not to take it!
I know!
Listen! I knew something sinister was at work here!
Sounds like the Dragonfly gang.
PROP CLOSET
Those rotten ankle-biters!
It's a really valuable painting!
How was I supposed to know?
PROP CLOS
Or it's the Termite Twosome!
Those no-good bloodsuckers!

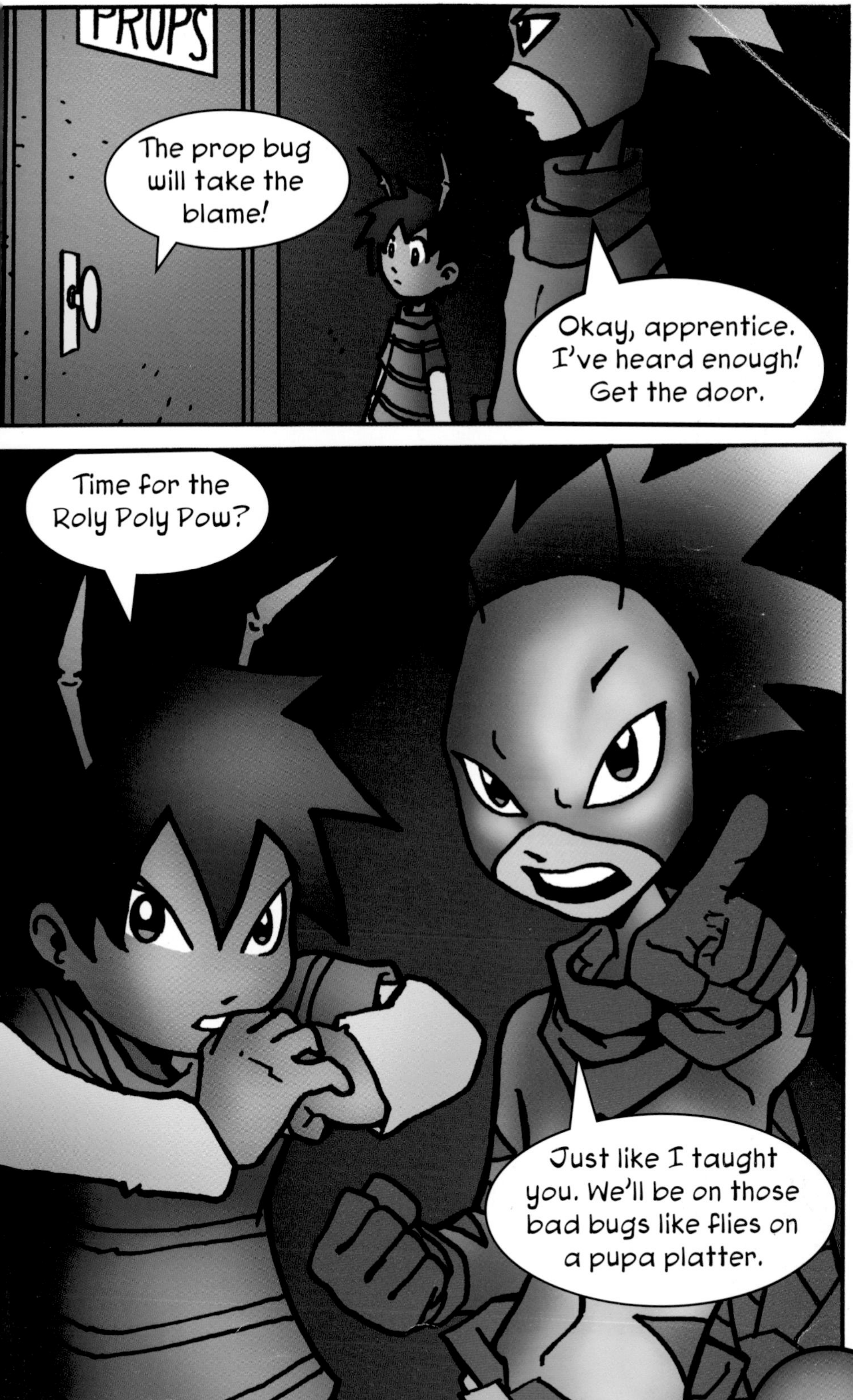
PROPS
The prop bug will take the blame!
Okay, apprentice. I've heard enough! Get the door.
Time for the Roly Poly Pow?
Just like I taught you. We'll be on those bad bugs like flies on a pupa platter.

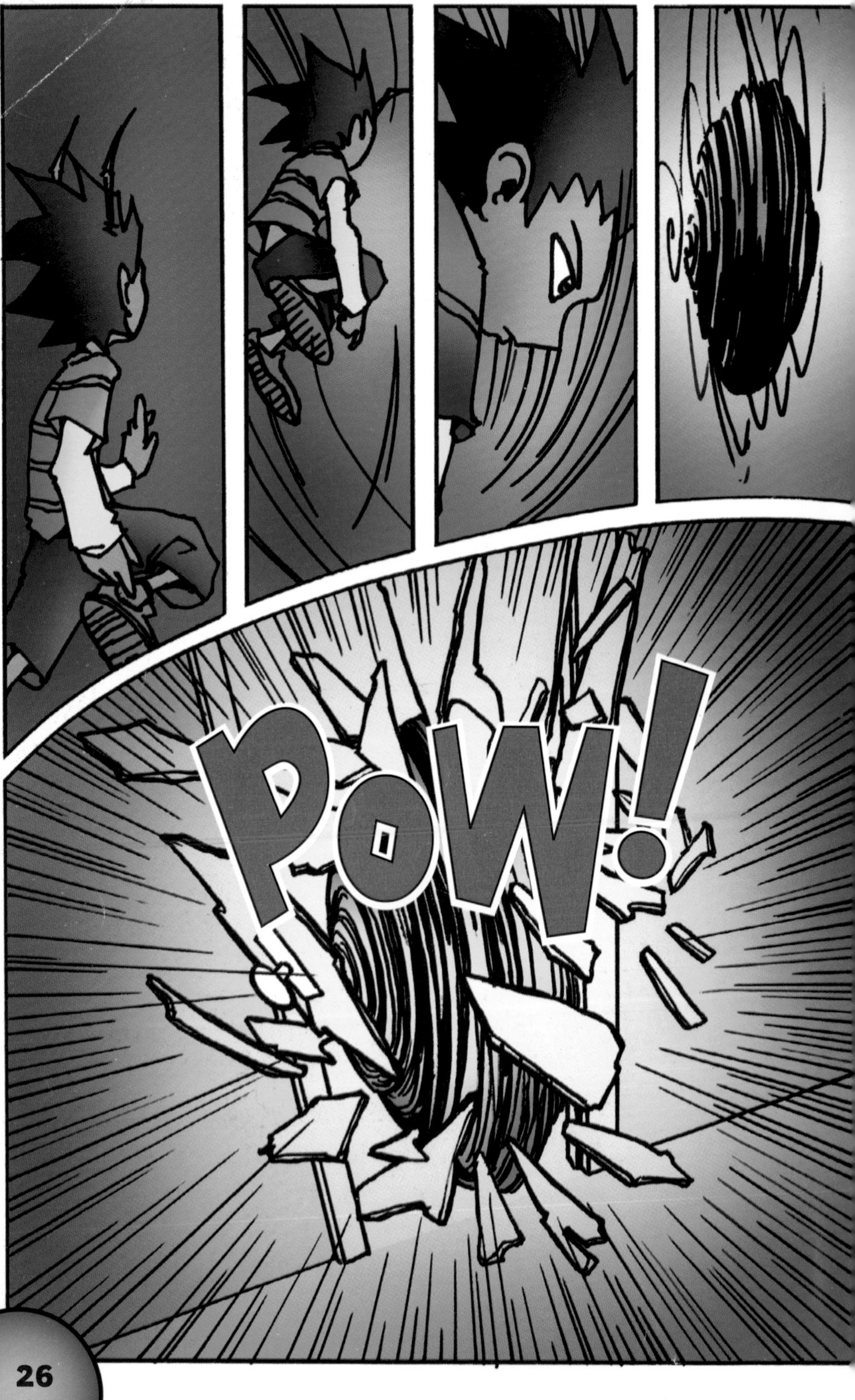
POW!

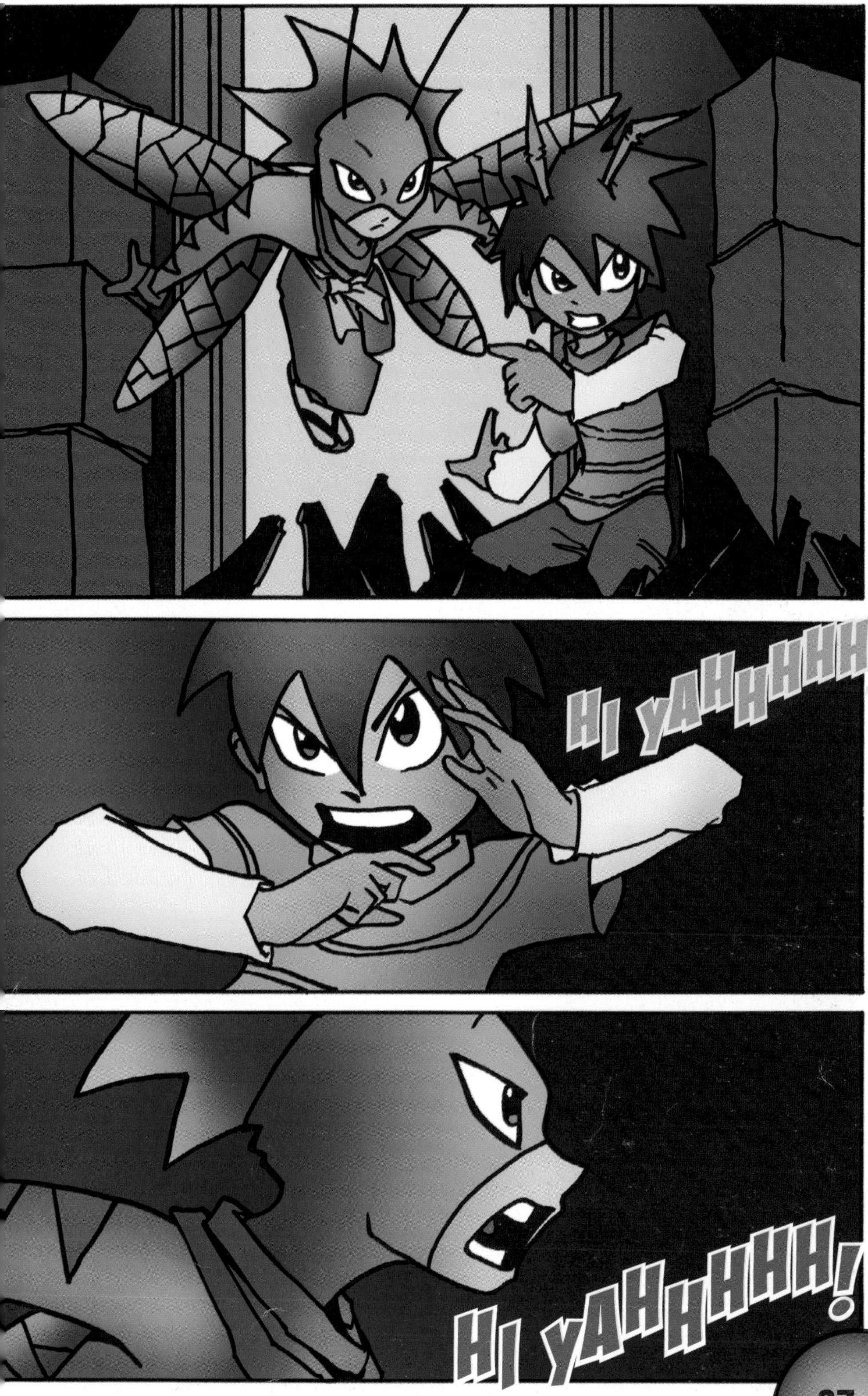
HI YAHHHHH!
HI YAHHHHH!

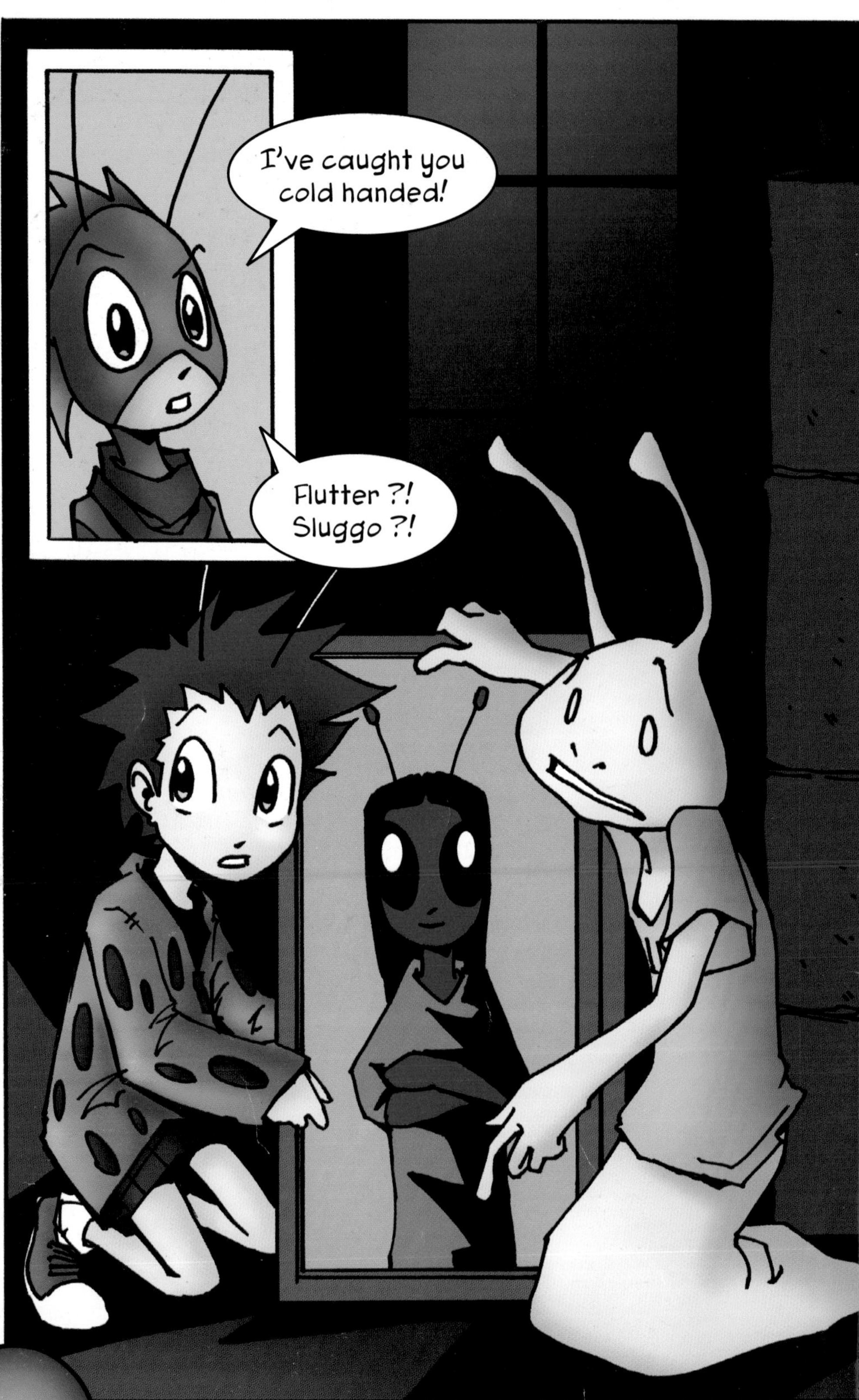
I've caught you cold handed!
Flutter ?! Sluggo ?!

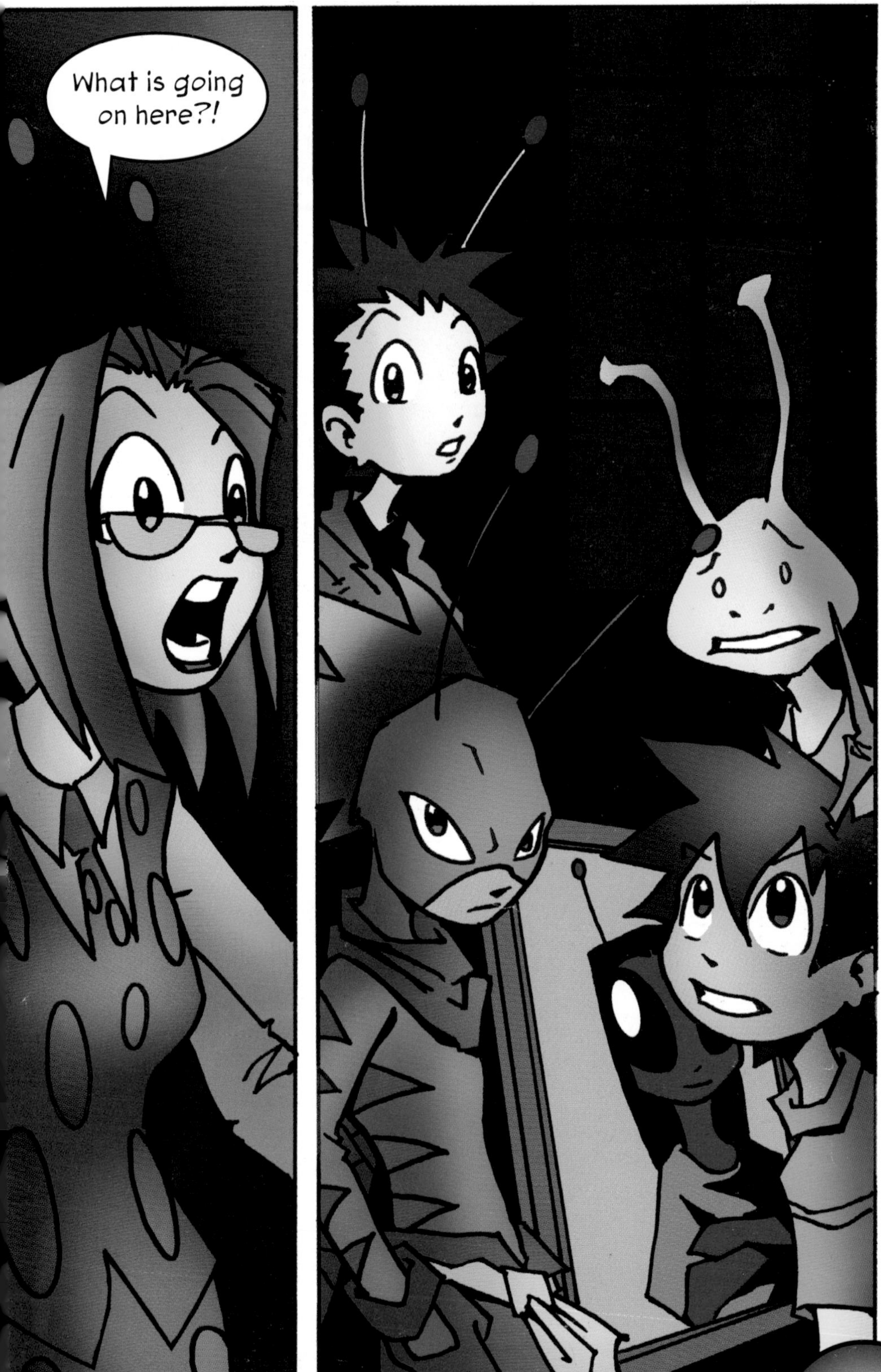
What is going on here?!

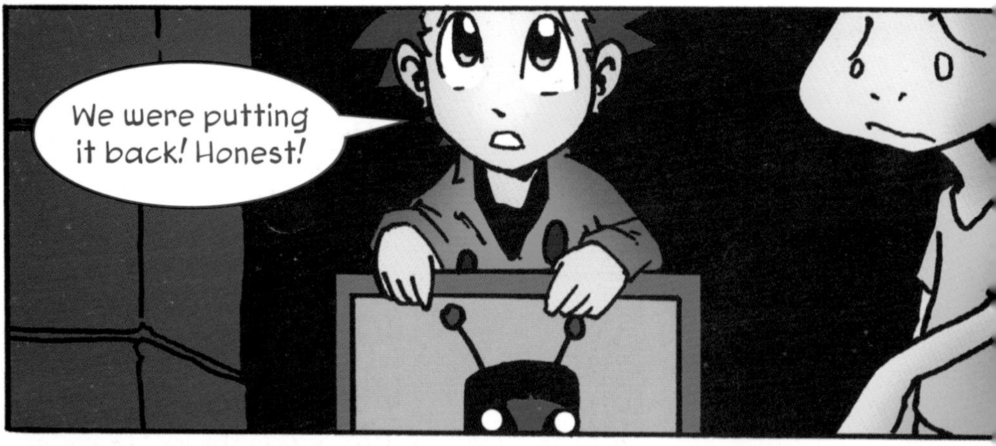
We were putting it back! Honest!

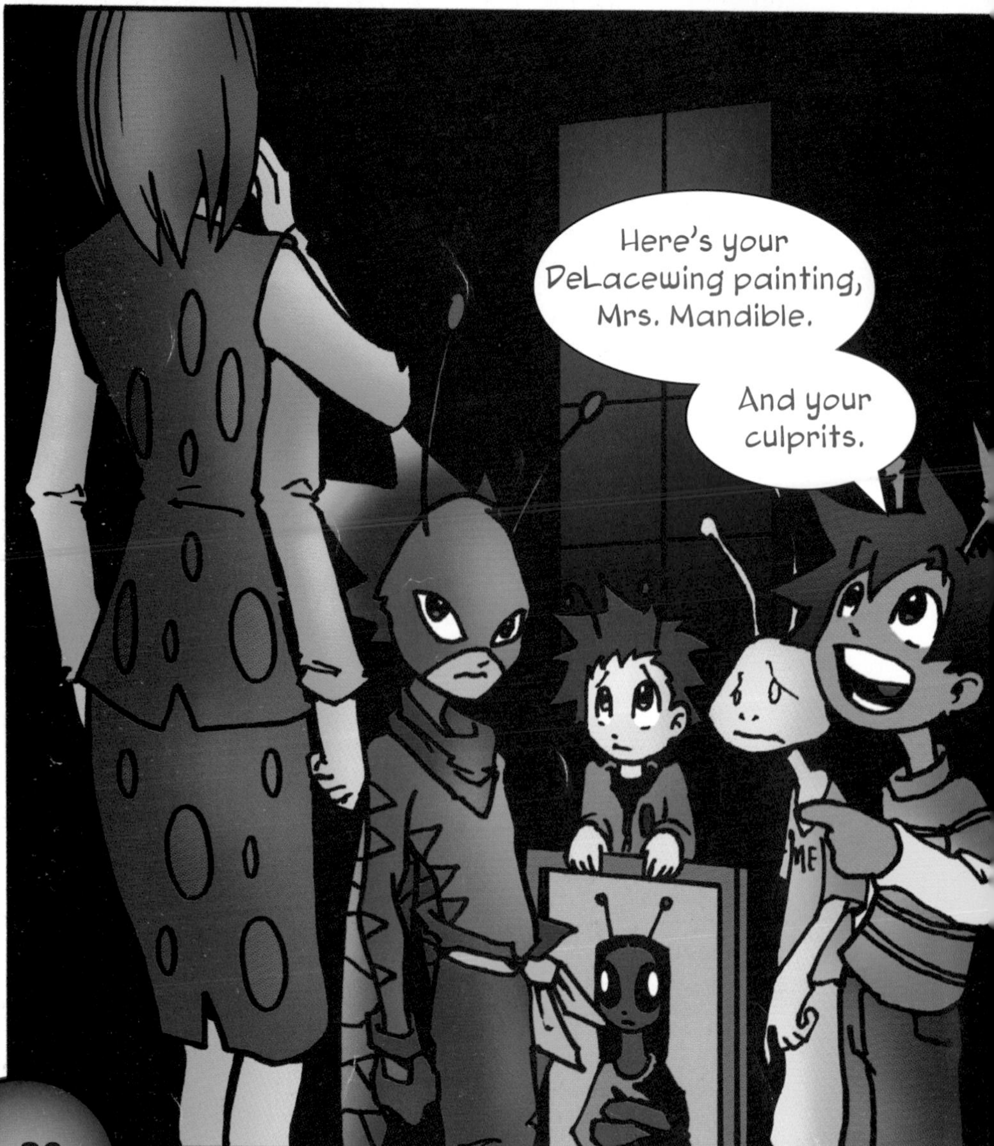
Here's your DeLacewing painting, Mrs. Mandible.
And your culprits.
ME

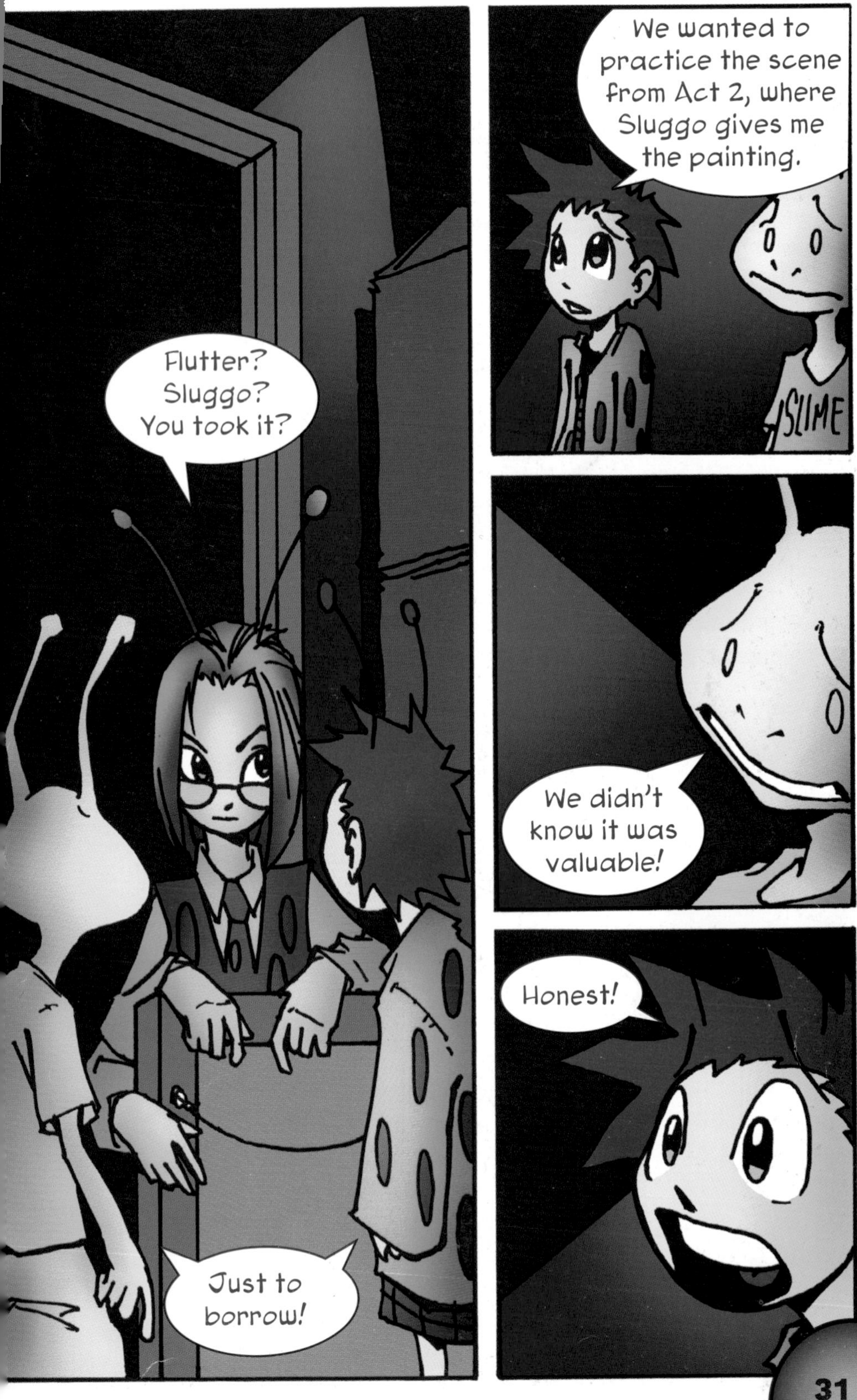
Flutter? Sluggo? You took it?
Just to borrow!
We wanted to practice the scene from Act 2, where Sluggo gives me the painting.
SLIME
We didn't know it was valuable!
Honest!

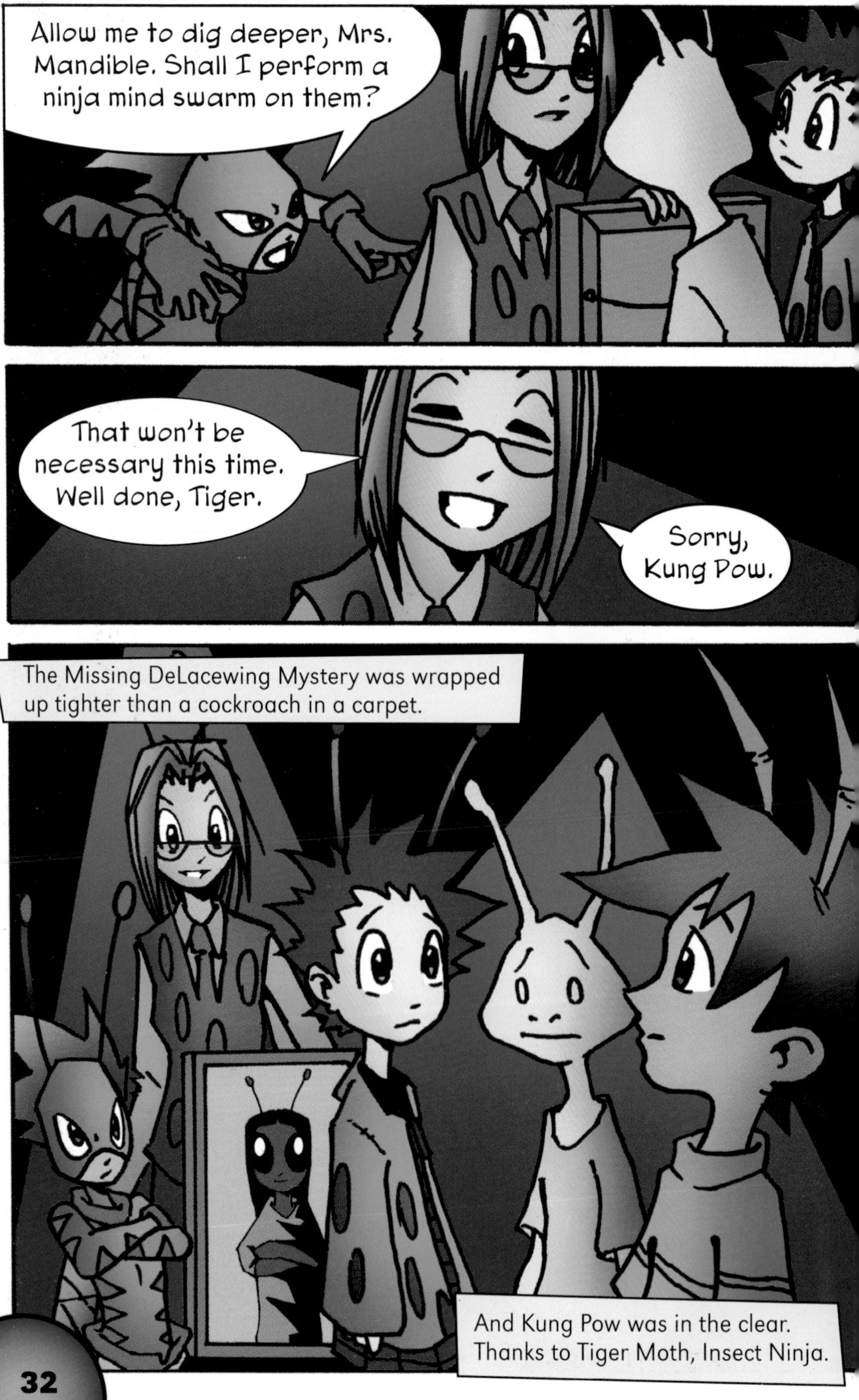
Allow me to dig deeper, Mrs. Mandible. Shall I perform a ninja mind swarm on them?
That won't be necessary this time. Well done, Tiger.
Sorry, Kung Pow.
The Missing DeLacewing Mystery was wrapped up tighter than a cockroach in a carpet.
And Kung Pow was in the clear. Thanks to Tiger Moth, Insect Ninja.

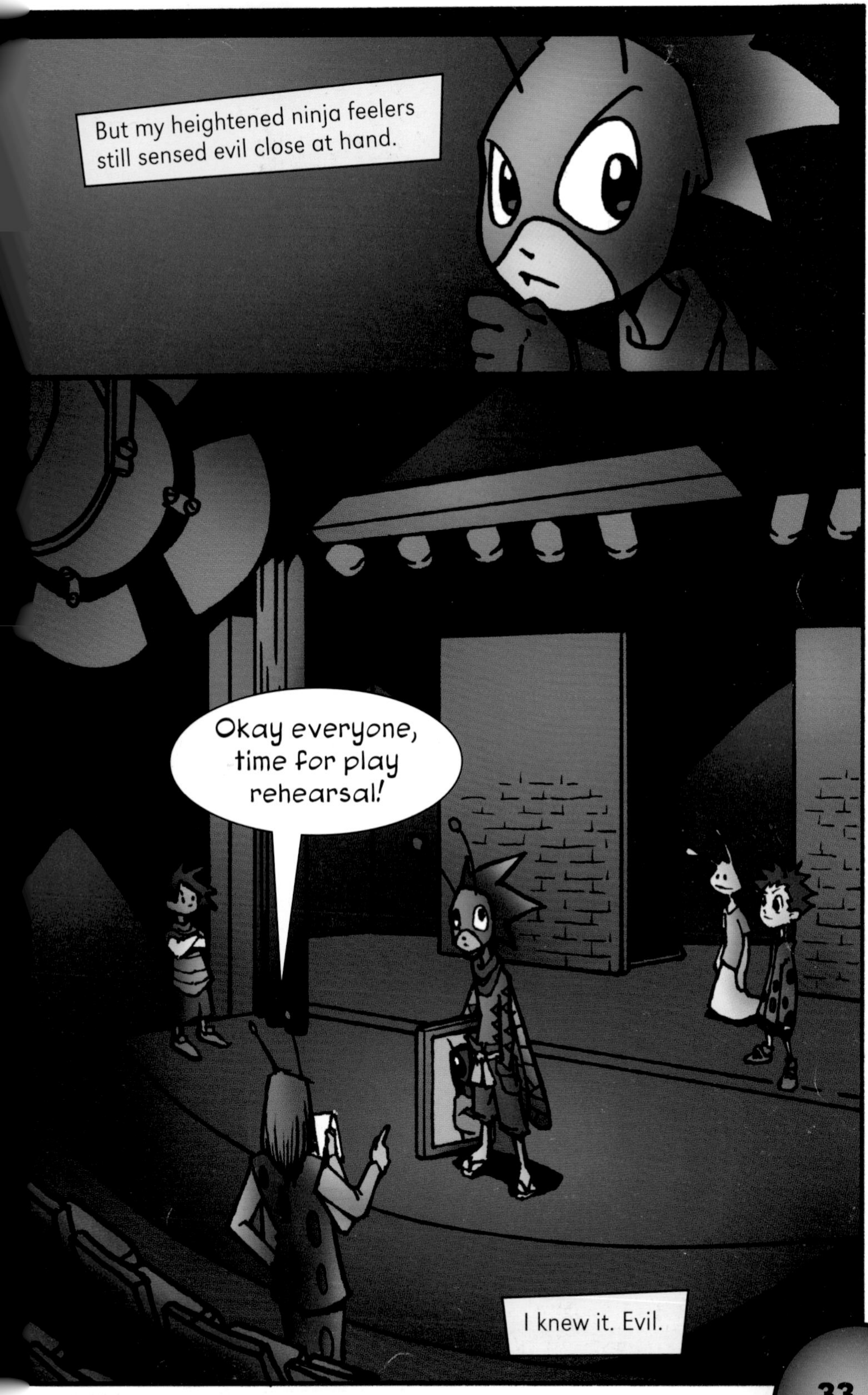
But my heightened ninja feelers still sensed evil close at hand.
Okay everyone, time for play rehearsal!
I knew it. Evil.

About the Author

Aaron Reynolds loves bugs and loves books, so Tiger Moth was a perfect blend of both. Aaron is the author of several great books for kids, including *Chicks and Salsa*, which *Publishers Weekly* called "a literary fandango" that "even confirmed macaroni-and-cheese lovers will devour." Aaron had no idea what a "fandango" was, but after looking it up in the dictionary, he hopes to write several more fandangos in the future. He lives near Chicago with his wife, two kids, and four insect-obsessed cats.

About the Illustrator

Erik Lervold was born in Puerto Rico, a small island in the Caribbean, and has been a professional painter. He attended college at the University of Puerto Rico's Mayaguez campus, where he majored in Civil Engineering. Deciding that he wanted to be a full-time artist, he moved to Florida, New York, Chicago, Duluth, and finally Minneapolis. He attended the Minneapolis College of Art and Design, majored in Comic Art, and graduated in 2004. Erik teaches classes in libraries in the Minneapolis area, and has taught art in the Minnesota Children's Museum. He loves the color green and has a bunch of really big goggles. He also loves sandwiches. If you want him to be your friend, bring him a roast beef sandwich and he will love you forever.

Glossary

apprentice (uh-PREN-tiss)—a person learning skills from another person who already knows them

authenticity (aw-then-TISS-it-ee)—being real and not a fake or a copy. A painting has authenticity if it was painted by a real artist.

culprits (KUHL-prits)—people who are guilty

exoskeleton (eks-oh-SKEL-uh-tuhn)—a hard protective structure on the outside of the body (imagine your ribs on the outside!). Insects have exoskeletons.

hi yahhhh (hi YAHHHH)—a noise made when breaking down a door and surprising thieves

maggots (MAG-uhts)—the eggs of houseflies

ninja (NIN-juh)—a person trained in the ancient method of Japanese martial arts. Ninjas usually don't like acting in school plays.

parasite (PARE-uh-site)—a living thing that lives on or in another living thing, like fleas on a dog. Ewww!

unsavory (uhn-SAY-vuh-ree)—something that has a bad taste or smell. Don't ever use the word "unsavory" when you're eating dinner at a friend's house!

From the Ninja Notebook: Undercover Insects

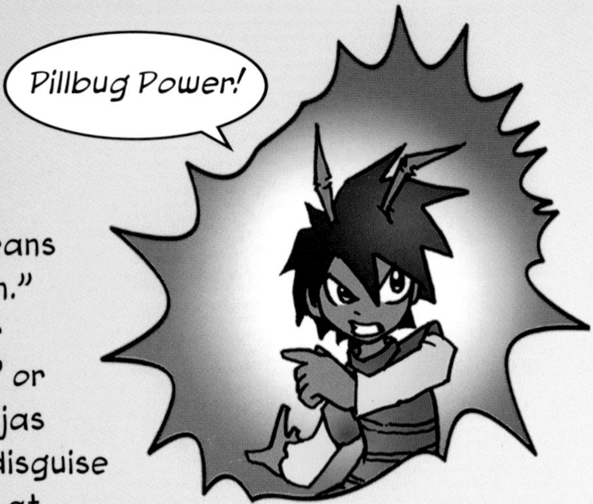
Pillbug Power!

The word Ninja means "the art of stealth." Stealth is another word for "secret" or "undercover." Ninjas were masters of disguise and were experts at hiding and blending in with their surroundings. Lots of insects do the same thing. They hide or disguise themselves to keep from being eaten by larger creatures.

The Indian dead-leaf butterfly can hide in the open. Once the butterfly folds its wings, it looks like a dead leaf. No one would want to eat it for dinner!

The walking stick insect looks just like a twig or a small branch.

Small, yellow crab spiders sit on sunflowers where they blend in with the bright petals. When a bee zooms in to visit the flower, the hidden spider pounces. It catches the bee and drags it behind the flower to feast.

The caterpillar of the hawk moth looks like a snake. This fake snake scares away any hungry birds that might be hunting for a tasty moth.

The carpenter moth has wings the color of tree bark. When the insect rests on a tree, it opens its wings wide and seems to disappear against the tree trunk.

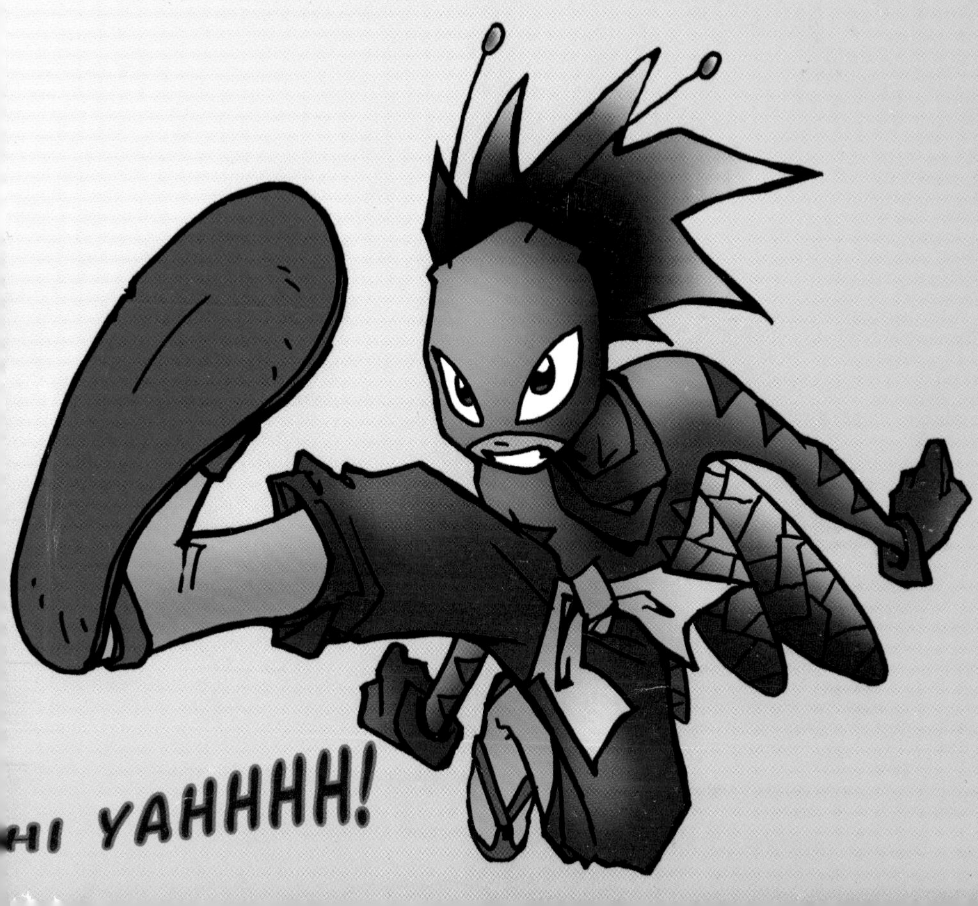
HI YAHHHH!

Discussion Questions

1. Just as Tiger Moth had to be in the school play, sometimes you have to participate in something you don't want to do. What school activities don't you like and why? What are some ways to deal with an unpleasant activity?

2. If your friend was accused of stealing, but you knew that your friend was innocent, what would you do to help?

3. Kung Pow was almost blamed for stealing. Have you ever been blamed for something you didn't do? How did it make you feel and why?

Writing Prompts

1. Imagine that you are a super hero. What would your name be? What would your super power be? Like Tiger Moth, who would you save, and what would you save them from? When you're finished writing, try drawing your super hero.

2. Mrs. Mandible has a painting that's special to her. What possession is special to you? How would you feel if it were lost or stolen?

Internet Sites

Do you want to know more about subjects related to this book? Or are you interested in learning about other topics? Then check out FactHound, a fun, easy way to find Internet sites.

Our investigative staff has already sniffed out great sites for you!

Here's how to use FactHound:

1. Visit www.facthound.com

2. Select your grade level.

3. To learn more about subjects related to this book, type in the book's ISBN number: **1598890573**.

4. Click the **Fetch It** button.

FactHound will fetch the best Internet sites for you!